Howling
Elke B

Elke Bergsma
Howling Offshore

EAST FRISIAN CRIME

copyright: © 2024 Elke Bergsma, www.elke-bergsma.de.
Am alten Handelshafen 1, 26789 Leer, Germany
title of the original German version: Wellenschlag
editing: Kanut Kirches, www.lektorat-kanut-kirches.de
cover: Susanne Elsen, www.mohnrot.com
using a photograph by ©andrejs polivanovs/shutterstock
translation: deepl.com
proofreading English version: Debbie Epstein
layout: Corinna Rindlisbacher, www.ebokks.de
ISBN: 9798329034028
Imprint: Independently published

Elke Bergsma grew up in East Frisia, Germany, in the wonderful expanse of countryside characterised by windmills, lighthouses, dykes, sheep and cows. Inspired by the books of Enid Blyton, she decided to become a writer. Some 30 years later she published her first novel. Out of love for her homeland and its inhabitants, she decided to write East Frisian crime novels and now does this full-time, passionately and successfully. Her German crime thrillers have sold more than 2 million copies. A lifelong dream came true.

For Debbie
thank you for being you

1

"Cape Town?" David Büttner thought he hadn't heard right. "Why on earth does it have to be Cape Town of all places?!"

"Because it's cool?" Jette didn't let the horror in her father's voice rattle her, but calmly continued spooning her dessert.

"That may be so, but … Cape Town? Really?" When Jette, who had recently graduated, had told him on the phone the day before that she had concrete plans for the next few months, he had thought of an internship, maybe a trip through Europe with friends. Just something harmless. He eyed his daughter, who had arrived unexpectedly from Bremen that morning, suspiciously. Was she pulling his leg?

Probably not, because she now said: "I have already booked the flight ticket. I have also already found a teacher. Debbie. My English is all rusty. It's about time I brush up on it."

"You can also learn English in England. You don't have to fly halfway around the world to do it."

Jette grimaced. "Oh, Pops."

"What's it about?" asked Susanne, who returned after leaving the kitchen for a moment. She sat down, whereupon Trude the cat saw her chance and jumped onto her lap.

"Cape Town," Jette mumbled, her mouth full of ice cream with hot cherries.

"I see."

"Oh?" Büttner looked at his wife in consternation. "You knew about that?"

"Yes. Jette told me earlier. You were still at work." She tickled Trude, who stretched her neck towards her, on the throat.

Büttner threw the kitchen towel he had just wiped his mouth with onto the table. "And why do you act so unconcerned all the time? I mean … it's Cape Town! Our daughter is not planning a trip to Sauerland, Susanne, but to South Africa!"

Susanne sighed, "Well, thank God it's not Sauerland, David, as beautiful as it is. But Cape Town is a lot more interesting than Lüdenscheid, as even you have to admit. So, I think it's a good plan."

"What's good about it?!" His wife's equanimity drove Büttner up the wall. "Just recently a tourist was murdered in South Africa! It was even reported on television!"

"You can die anywhere," Jette replied soberly. She pushed her empty dessert bowl aside. "You of all people should know that Pops".

"Hm." He didn't know what to say to this allusion to his job. "And how long do you plan to stay in Cape Town?"

"Three months. Maybe four if I like it there. I have time, as you know."

Yes, he knew that. Jette would not start her job as a research assistant at the University of Bremen until the new semester in April, and there were still five months to go. In that respect, he had to admit, the idea of slipping away to the southern hemisphere was not a bad one at all, because it would allow her to avoid the local winter and enjoy a second summer. Still … the thought of his daughter being so far away did not please him at all. If something really happened to her or if she needed help, it would be ages before he was with her. A nightmare. "How many hours does it take to fly there?" he asked.

"From Frankfurt, just under twelve," Jette answered. "Why? Are you planning a weekend trip?" She grinned broadly.

"And when do you want to start?" He ignored this tip.

"Tomorrow."

"Tomorrow?" Büttner swallowed hard.

"Yes. I got a cheap flight at short notice. So, what else should I wait for?" She pointed up at the ceiling. "Already brought my luggage. It's in my room."

"Do … do you even have a place to stay yet?" In his imagination, he saw Jette stranded in one of those miserable townships.

"I'm staying with Debbie. She lives in a cute little house not far from the beach and is renting me a room."

"The English teacher? But you don't even know her!"

Jette looked at him frowning. "I don't know if you know it, Pops, but people can be met."

"I think this solution is great," Susanne said. "This way, Jette has someone to speak English with all day. It couldn't be more perfect.

Büttner snorted indignantly. Debbie or not, he could think of a whole lot of circumstances that would be more perfect than his daughter staying on the other side of the world. "And why are you only now letting us in on your plans? I mean …"

"That's exactly why," Susanne interrupted him impatiently. "Because you can't accept that your daughter is grown up and makes her own decisions." She patted his arm conciliatory. "Now just be happy for her, David! Cape Town must be gorgeous, I hear. I wouldn't mind visiting her there for a few days. We could combine it with a safari in the Kruger National Park, what do you think?" Her look took on something rapturous. "I've always wanted to go there."

"On a safari?" Büttner contorted his face in agony. "I really don't know what's so desirable about staring after a few wild animals. And it's not entirely safe either." He frowned. "Are you planning to go there alone, Jette, or is Kai going with you?"

"Nah. Kai doesn't have time. He doesn't get a holiday for that long. But he'll come to visit me, I think. Maybe over Christmas and New Year."

Büttner's jaw dropped. "You're not here for Christmas?"

Susanne crossed her arms and looked at him, shaking her head. "If you could do maths, you wouldn't have asked that question, David. Of course she won't be here at Christmas. How could she be?"

Büttner rose from his seat. "Time for a glass of red wine," he decided. This shock needed to be digested first. "Would you like one too?"

"At this hour?" Susanne shook her head. "I still want to go into town, I have a date. Ask me again tonight."

As Büttner rummaged in a drawer for a corkscrew, his

smartphone began to ring shrilly. He looked at the display and answered the call. "What's up, Hasenkrug?"

"A corpse," his assistant replied. "In Greetsiel."

"Stupid." Büttner looked regretfully at the red wine, which would probably have to wait until the evening after all. "Wait for me, Hasenkrug, I'll come to the police station, then we'll set off together. Do we know anything more?"

"Except that it appears to be a young woman."

"Okay. Be right there." He hung up.

Susanne looked at him with interest. "A new case?"

"Yes. Body found in Greetsiel."

"Greetsiel." Jette pursed her mouth mockingly. "So much for 'Cape Town is sooo dangerous, Jette'! Honestly? I would say that East Frisia can easily keep up with you as far as the murder rate is concerned. Funnily enough, you've never warned me not to come here."

Since his chain of arguments was now threatening to become even more full of holes, Büttner preferred to go on his way. No one seemed to want to listen to him here after all.

2

"Cape Town? Cool!" Sebastian Hasenkrug nodded appreciatively.

David Büttner sighed as if he were carrying the weight of the whole world on his shoulders. "I should have guessed that you would once again close your mind to logical thinking, Hasenkrug. But wait until your daughter grows up and leaves for South Africa for several months. Then you won't think Cape Town is cool either, I bet." He switched the windscreen wipers of his company car to the next higher setting. Coming from the North Sea, a cold north-westerly storm swept unchecked across the flat, desolate land, driving the rain mercilessly against the windscreen. Driving across the Krummhörn in this East Frisian autumn weather was no pleasure.

"Children grow up, boss. Should we lock them up so they stay with us forever?"

"If you ask me, Hasenkrug, we should never have let her out of the car seat." Büttner thought wistfully back to the time when Jette had marvelled at the world from her car seat and he had shown her everything. But with every step she learned to take on her own, with every skill she acquired, she had needed him a little less. And now she had long since grown up. Where had the time gone?

"I understand that it is difficult," Hasenkrug said conciliatory. "And I certainly won't be doing a dance of joy when my children leave the nest. Although sometimes I do feel a sense of anticipation for this day. For example, when Mara gets her princess airs again or I can just prevent Silas from burning down the whole house with his friends."

"Believe me, you will wish all this back when the time comes." Büttner himself didn't know why he was so deep in self-pity right now. Maybe it was the dreary November weather, maybe it was because he hadn't even been allowed a glass of red wine after the horror. In any case, the fact was that a little cheering up would have done him good. But a corpse in Greetsiel would probably not be able to do that. "Where do we have to go?" he asked as they approached the fishing village.

"To the harbour," Hasenkrug replied. "The news just came in that it's a floater."

This did not exactly raise Büttner's spirits, because a floater was not a nice sight to see. He turned off towards the twin mills of Greetsiel and headed for the cutter harbour. There was unusually little activity on the streets of the fishing village. Only a few passers-by could be seen trudging through the rain with their heads down. Many shops also seemed to be closed, with no lights on behind most of the shop windows. The contrast to the warm season was enormous. If you got lost here in the summer, there was hardly any room to tip over on the streets, so densely packed were the holidaymakers pushing their way through the streets paved with red clinker bricks.

At the harbour, on the other hand, there was a lot going on when Büttner parked the car at the Hotel *Hohes Haus.*

"Where do all these people come from?" wondered Hasenkrug. "I always thought Greetsiel hardly had any inhabitants. And there shouldn't be too many tourists here at the moment."

"I wonder what's driving them out of their houses in this weather." Büttner shuddered at the mere thought of being defenceless against rain and storm in a moment. "A body in the dry would have been nice too," he muttered as he reached for the back seat where he had put his mackintosh.

In fact, there seemed to be several dozen people who had gathered at the dock. Several patrol colleagues tried hard to push the onlookers back behind the barriers that had been set up, but for some reason they seemed to actively resist them.

"Well, they're really up in arms," Hasenkrug observed, as a man in heavy oilskins attacked a policeman with his fists raised. Büttner assumed that it was one of the crab fishermen, as the rowdy was wearing one of those orange waders that fishermen wore on the high seas.

Büttner switched the engine on again and with it the windscreen wipers and the ventilation.

Hasenkrug, who had leaned over to see better through the wet and steamed-up window, looked at his boss in irritation. "Are you trying to get away again?"

"Nah, I want to see something." For a while, Büttner watched the action through the windscreen. "There seem to be two camps," he finally observed. "Like at one of those demos when right-wing and left-wing activists go at each other because they think violence is a proven way to beat the other side's own views into their brains." To his regret, he could not understand what the angry people were about because of the noisy weather.

"The colleagues have called for reinforcements," Hasenkrug announced after he had focused on the police radio. "Two squad cars are on their way here."

"Well," Büttner leaned back in his seat, "let's let our colleagues do their work before we jump into the fray. I don't feel like getting a fist in the face from one of the punchers. But if you want to get involved, Hasenkrug …" he made an inviting gesture with his hand, "here you go."

The intervention of the colleagues, who soon arrived with flashing lights, did not take as long as expected. Obviously, some of the rioters got pissed off when the officers jumped out of the vans. At least half of the people who had been shouting and chanting their fists in the air scattered in all directions, quite a few stumbled and slid down the dike between the picturesque Frisian houses. Presumably they did not care to have their personal details taken.

There were only two scuffles between passers-by and police officers in the next few minutes, but otherwise the haunting, which seemed strangely surreal in the idyll of Greetsiel, came to a quick end. Over the radio, Hasenkrug asked his colleagues to continue to secure the harbour, otherwise they would not be able to deal with the murder case properly.

Together with Büttner and Hasenkrug, the forensic team led by Chris Bäumler arrived.

"You've been standing around here for quite a while," Bäumler noted as he walked next to Büttner in the direction of the crab boats rocking restlessly in the harbour basin. "Do you have any idea what that was all about?"

"Nah. But we'll find out for sure," replied Büttner, who was busy tightening the hood of his mackintosh under his chin. The storm tugged at their clothes even harder out here on the coast than it had done in the city. "It's not going to be easy for you," he said.

"Dozens of fresh DNA around the crime scene, plus endless water from above and below ... that doesn't look good." Bäumler sighed. "Not to mention the corpse, which the salt water has certainly given a thorough full-body peeling. I'm afraid the report we're going to give you will be a very manageable one, David."

They reached the quay wall. The noise caused by the vibrating shrouds, the rattling clickers and the squeaking fenders due to the wind was enormous.

"Where is the body?" inquired Büttner. He looked around the quay wall, but nothing resembling a corpse could be seen far and wide.

A fisherman standing next to him, also in orange waders and rubber boots, pointed out to the water between the boats lying in packs of three. "There, by the green cutter. Must have got caught somewhere."

"She hasn't been recovered yet?" Büttner contorted his face as if he suddenly had a toothache. With each wave – and there were quite a few – the body was smashed against the hull of the cutter again and again.

"Okay, we can definitely forget about finding any useful traces on the corpse," Chris Bäumler remarked sourly. "But maybe Anja Wilkens can still do something with her."

Anja Wilkens. Büttner looked around but could not see the forensic doctor anywhere. "Has she even been notified yet?"

"She was," said Hasenkrug. "But she had another case to review."

"Another homicide?" asked Chris Bäumler.

"Nah. Domestic violence."

"Whatever," Büttner said to his uniformed colleagues, who were standing there waiting, "now see to it that you fish the body out of the water. I assume photos have already been taken?" He looked up at the sky, where black clouds were rolling in. "It won't be long now before it's dark."

"Yes," growled the uniformed man, water running down his clothes. "Photos are taken. It was damn rough on the cutter. That's why we asked our colleagues from the fire brigade to help us salvage it. They should be here any minute."

"Do they already know who the dead woman is?" Hasenkrug inquired.

"Gina," was the curt reply.

Büttner expected further information, but he only mentioned her first name. "Just make sure you don't tell us too much," he growled indignantly.

For a few seconds, the colleague looked at him perplexed, but then it seemed to dawn on him that this instruction could be meant ironically. He cleared his throat. "Gina Gloger, nineteen years old, living with her parents in Greetsiel, graduated from the Gymnasium in Norden this year."

"That means her parents already know about their daughter's death?"

"Yes. They are at home. We have requested a grief counselor to look after them. I told them you'd come by later."

"Okay." Büttner couldn't say he was particularly eager for the visit, but it probably couldn't be avoided. "You know the family?"

"No, not really. But Eiko," he pointed to a colleague who was talking to a fisherman standing on one of the cutters, "he knows the Glogers well. Always has, he says. Because his father is also a fisherman. Just like his brother. And Gina's father, of course. And the fishing families, they know each other in Greetsiel."

"Eiko is the odd one out in the family, it seems to me."

"Yup. He's not so much into fishing." The colleague wiped the rain off his face. "But when there's a need and Eiko doesn't have a shift, he goes out with us. He's learned all that, too. Before he went to the police, I mean."

"How long has he been with the Emden police?" Büttner could not remember ever having seen him or having had an assignment with him.

"Not long. A few weeks ago. He got himself transferred from Norden to Emden after Gina broke up with him. He's got a flat in Emden now, too."

Büttner listened up. "That means he was involved with our victim?"

"Yeah. They lived together. In Norden."

Okay, this information could have come a little earlier, Büttner thought, but since two emergency vehicles of the volunteer fire brigade were arriving, he refrained from making a remark to that effect.

By the time the body had been recovered at great expense, daylight had departed. On the quay were floodlights that bathed the harbour in a harsh white light. The resulting, mostly wavering shadows of the ships' superstructures and the moving people had a ghostly effect.

Büttner looked more closely at the young woman with the unattractively dislocated limbs. He estimated her to be about one metre seventy. She was of slender build and dressed appropriately for the season. Her long blonde hair, with all sorts of vegetable matter caught in it, stickily framed her completely battered face. Impossible to say whether she had been pretty in the vernacular sense or not, they would have to look at a photograph of her.

"Does she have papers or her mobile phone with her?" he asked.

"No, nothing," replied a fireman who looked visibly upset and was lighting a cigarette. "We checked right away. But it's Gina, no doubt about it." He inhaled a deep drag. "Shit, man. She didn't deserve that."

"You knew her?"

"Yeah. Shit, man." He noisily expelled the smoke, but it swirled right back around his face. "You really don't need that, having to pull a dead person you know out of the water."

"Please leave your contact details with my colleagues," Büttner told him as the firefighter moved away. He raised his hand in confirmation.

In the meantime, Dr. Anja Wilkens had also arrived and immediately bent over the corpse while the flash of a camera flashed around her as soon as the police photographer pressed the shutter release of his camera. "Phew," she said not much later, "there's hardly a bone left intact on her, it seems to me."

"Could it be from the constant collision with the cutter?" inquired Hasenkrug. "Or were her bones broken before she died?"

"I don't know yet. I'll be able to tell you more after the autopsy. It's not impossible that it's both."

"How long do you reckon she's been dead?"

"She wasn't in the water for too long. I'd guess twenty hours at the most." She examined the body more closely. "Hm, I could imagine that she drowned."

"Fully conscious?", Büttner wanted to know.

"Possibly. But more on that later, too." She rose from her crouch and brushed the disposable gloves off her hands. "There, that's about it for my part. As soon as I get them on the table, I'll get to work. You'll have my report tomorrow." She gathered up her stuff and walked away quickly.

"Are we going to the relatives now?" asked Hasenkrug.

"No." Büttner shook his head. He had decided against it after a moment's thought. "They have a chaplain to look after them. Let's give them the time. It's enough if we talk to them tomorrow. I assume we have the contact details of all the relevant witnesses?"

Hasenkrug nodded. "I assume so."

Büttner pointed to the patrol car, into which his colleagues had meanwhile loaded the two men who were ready to strike. "What about those two?"

"We'll take her to the police station." Hasenkrug grinned. "To cool off."

"Good. Once they're running at normal temperature

again, why don't you ask them what all the action was about?"

"There are already a few statements that the colleagues have taken down. We can evaluate them first thing in the morning and then see what happens." Hasenkrug also did not seem to attach any great importance to taking action today. Büttner could only agree with him. He himself just wanted to go home and put on dry clothes. But above all, he wanted to spend the evening with Jette.

Cape Town. He shook his head inwardly. What a stupid idea.

3

"Cape Town?" Marieluise Weniger rolled her eyes in delight. "Hach, I've always wanted to go there. It must be beautiful, I hear. I envy Jette deeply. But how nice for her to have this opportunity, don't you think?"

David Büttner let out an undefined grumble. Apparently, he could not hope for too much solidarity regarding his opinion of Jette's travel plans. He took the cup of coffee from his secretary's hand, which she held out to him. "Is your colleague here yet?"

"You mean Eiko Harms? Yes, he is already sitting in your office with colleague Hasenkrug." She looked sadly at the recently acquired coffee machine, which for some reason was making gurgling noises. "The death of his ex-girlfriend seems to have hit him inthe stomach. He even spurned the coffee from this fantastic machine. He just wanted to drink a cup of chamomile tea."

"Hm." Büttner had only listened with half an ear. Saying goodbye to Jette that morning had been so difficult for him that he had barely been able to hold back his tears. But of course he had not wanted to deprive her of the euphoria she had already exuded the previous evening when she had imagined in the most colourful terms what a fantastic time she would have in Cape Town. Now she was on her way to

Frankfurt airport by train. As nice as it was to see what a self-confident person Jette had become, it was also hard to let her go. If she had at least not travelled alone to the other end of the world, but had taken Kai with her, then …

Büttner admonished himself to concentrate on his job and entered his office.

"Chief?"

"Huh?" Büttner caught himself drifting off in thought again.

"I said hello." Sebastian Hasenkrug looked at him scrutinisingly.

"Er… yes… Moin."

"Are you all right, boss?"

"Yeah, sure, what's up?" Büttner nodded to Eiko Harms, who also murmured a Moin, and sat down at his desk.

"Let's be clear," Harms said without being asked, "I had nothing to do with Gina's death." He raised his hand, which was trembling slightly, as if to swear. "Nothing, I swear."

"Has anyone said otherwise?" asked Büttner.

"Nah … er … well … nah. Not exactly." The young colleague scratched his head in embarrassment. "I just thought I'd better say it now. Don't want me to get suspicious around here or anything. I could never do anything to Gina. Never."

Büttner eyed the man, who, dressed in his uniform, was sitting on a chair in front of his desk with his elongated legs stretched out, appraisingly. He was in his mid-twenties, slim, obviously well-toned, his blond hair cut stubble short. His facial skin was that of someone who spent a lot of time in the fresh air at any time of year. Harms' cheeks glowed red, a vein throbbed in his neck, which might have been due to excitement. When he lifted his gaze and looked directly at Büttner, the deep sadness in his eyes was impossible to miss. "D-do we know … a-so w-do we already know what exactly happened to Gina … well, what happened?" he stuttered.

Büttner looked questioningly at Hasenkrug, who shook his head. Which either meant that the forensic department really did not have an autopsy report yet, or that the findings were not suitable for the ears of potential suspects.

Which in turn raised the question of how they intended to deal with Eiko Harms, because as a colleague it should be easy for him to get information on the murder case. Even if his superiors released him from duty for the time being, this was no guarantee that he would be cut off from the flow of information. Depending on Harms' relationship to his colleagues, one or the other could do him a favour in this regard.

However. It was up to others to decide how to proceed in this case, so it was unnecessary to worry about it now. He, Büttner, was primarily interested in Harms as a witness.

"When did you last see Gina Gloger?" he asked, reflecting on his real concern.

"Night before last."

"So the night before she was floating dead in the harbour basin."

"It wasn't me!" Panic flashed in Harms' eyes.

Büttner made a placating gesture with his hand. "I didn't say that either. Where did you meet Gina Gloger that evening?"

"We had an appointment. In … er… Greetsiel." It seemed to dawn on him that this was not exactly the place that would absolve him of any suspicion.

"What were you doing there?"

"A walk along the dyke, having an ice cream, chatting, that kind of thing."

"Was there a special reason for the meeting?"

Harms stared at his fingers, which he kneaded in his lap. "Gina had called me. She said she wanted to talk to me."

"So, what was it about?"

"I don't know. I … I think she was worried. She already sounded so strange on the phone."

"Worried?"

"Yeah. She looked at me funny a couple of times. As if she wanted to tell me what was bothering her. But then she shook her head and didn't say anything. So nothing important."

"According to that, she didn't really express to you that she was worried, right?", Büttner made sure.

"Yes, well no, not directly. But I saw it in her face. But then …", Harms shook his head. "I guess she didn't dare tell me the truth."

"The truth?", Büttner inquired. "About what?"

"I don't know. She didn't say anything." When Büttner looked at him frowning, Harms added: "Well, she didn't say why she was worried. Not even when I asked her directly. *Why are you worried?*" I asked. But she just shook her head and said she wasn't worried, and what made me think that and all." He sighed. "But I know it was different. And now," he made a jerky gesture with his hand, "and now what she was worried about, has happened He raised his eyes. "Or don't you think?"

Büttner came more and more to the conclusion that his young colleague was not exactly the brightest candle on the cake. It was hard to imagine that he would make much of a career in the police. But maybe that wasn't his goal at all.

"Did you meet more often after your separation?", Hasenkrug wanted to know.

Harms pressed his lips together. "Not as often as I wanted."

"And Gina? Did she see it the same way?" Büttner inquired. "Would she also have wanted more frequent meetings?"

Harms didn't have to answer to deny this because his facial expression said it all. "She … well Gina … she did," he looked at the ceiling and breathed in and out noisily. "She had someone else. I don't think she was happy with him though. Can't have been if you ask me. But it's best to ask him yourself what he did with her."

Büttner frowned. "What he did to her? What do you mean?"

"I don't know what she saw in him. I really don't." It didn't escape Büttner that Harms' hands clenched into fists. "He didn't do her any good. I'm sure of that."

Büttner lowered his head and looked up at him from below. "You are sure of this because …?"

"Because he's an asshole, that's why," it came back bluntly. "He always has been."

"Does *he* also have a name?" asked Hasenkrug.

"Jesko Mudder."

Hasenkrug's fingers slid over the keyboard. "Did Gina tell you that this Jesko is doing something to her?"

"Nah. She didn't have to. I knew that too. Because he's always been mean to women."

"Hm." Now this was not exactly the kind of statement that would convince the prosecutor and judge to bring charges against Jesko Mudder. Unless he had a criminal record for assault. Büttner suspected that that was exactly what Hasenkrug was trying to find out. "Can you imagine that it was Jesko Mudder who killed Gina?"

"Who else could it have been?" Harms' eyes narrowed to narrow slits. "If I get my hands on him, then … then …"

"… you'd better pull back very quickly," Büttner admonished him. "Or do you want to be the one who ultimately goes to jail?" He took a sip of coffee. "Now let's go back to your relationship with Gina Gloger, colleague Harms. How long were you involved with her?"

"A little more than a year."

"That's not very long."

"Nah."

"And how long ago did Gina break up with you?"

"Four months, three weeks and two days," it came like a shot from a pistol.

"And what was the reason?"

"Jesko. He was always picking on Gina."

"How exactly do we need to think about this?"

"Well, he showed up everywhere she was, danced with her, took her out for cocktails, gave her presents … that sort of thing."

"Until she finally let herself be wrapped up."

Harms nodded. "Jesko was up for it. But he didn't care about Gina at all. She was just a trophy for him. Because she was so pretty."

Büttner looked at his screen, on which Hasenkrug had shown him a photo of the young woman. Without a doubt, Gina had been as pretty as a picture with her slender figure, her long blonde hair, her full, heart-shaped mouth and almond-shaped eyes. Moreover, wearing a cropped top and holding her smartphone in her hand, she showed herself as flirtatious as could be seen a thousand times on social media. Apparently, she had posed for this photo in front of a mirror. Büttner wondered whether she really looked like that, or whether she had deliberately trimmed her body to fit the media by means of an image editing programme.

Büttner turned his screen so that Eiko Harms could see it too. "Did your ex-girlfriend look like that?"

Harms gasped briefly, obviously caught off guard by being confronted so unexpectedly with a photo of his ex-girlfriend. "Y-yes. That's Gina."

"Do you know for what purpose she took this picture?"

"For the internet, what else would it be for? I saw it on Instagram." Harms snorted. "But she wasn't like that before. She made herself an internet whore for Jesko so he'd think she was good."

"What was she like?"

"Well, she was … not so … so slutty. She was … all natural." Harms rubbed his fingers together nervously. "Until Jesko came along, she didn't want anything to do with all that shit, with Instagram and stuff."

When Hasenkrug signalled to him, Büttner turned his screen back towards him. Immediately afterwards, a picture appeared showing a young couple standing in front of a mirror. Judging by the background, it was the same mirror that had just been seen, and Gina was wearing the same clothes. The young woman had puckered her brightly made-up lips into a kissing mouth and was smiling provocatively at the camera. The man standing behind her held her possessively, his right tattooed arm resting under her breasts so that they were slightly raised. Hardly likely that this had happened accidentally.

Büttner turned the screen again. "Is that Jesko Mudder?"

Eiko Harms closed his eyes for a moment, visibly having to control himself. "Yes, that's the pig. I told you he turned Gina into a whore."

"But she doesn't seem to have minded," Hasenkrug noted provocatively, whereupon he was virtually stabbed by Harms' looks. "I just had a look on Instagram. She uploaded these photos herself. And several more in which she presents herself in … well, spicy positions."

"I already told you she wasn't like that!" Harms stuck his finger out towards the screen. "That asshole made her that way! Gina wasn't like that. She was completely different." It was obvious that he did not want to see her memory soiled in this way.

Hasenkrug played in a few more pictures, but Harms could no longer see them. In the next shot, Mudder's hand was on Gina's pubic bone, one click further between her legs. All in all, the display looked pornographic. Gina didn't give the impression of resisting it. But that could be deceptive, of course. Was this possibly the cause of the concern Harms thought he had noticed in her?

Following a hunch, Büttner asked: "You don't happen to have a photo with you that shows what Gina was like before she was with Josef …"

"Jesko," corrected Hasenkrug.

"Got together with Jesko?"

Eiko Harms fumbled a wallet out of the back pocket of his jeans, then pulled out a photo and handed it to Büttner. This picture showed him and Gina, also closely embraced, but in no way pornographic. Rather – against the backdrop of the Greetsiel crab cutter fleet – an apparently happy couple looked smilingly into the camera. Gina appeared to be wearing no make-up, or at best discreet make-up, and she also refrained from pursing her lips, instead smiling, and showing a row of even teeth. Her figure, however, was the same as in the Instagram pictures, so they did not appear to have been edited in that respect.

"When is this picture from?"

Harms shrugged his shoulders. "It's been just under a year, maybe."

"She has changed." And not to her advantage, Büttner added mentally.

"Told you."

"Do you have any idea if Gina wanted to meet with anyone yesterday?" asked Hasenkrug.

"No, I don't know anything. I would have said so long ago if I knew anything."

"Okay, colleague, that's it for now," said Büttner. "If we have any more questions …"

"Sure," Harms didn't let him finish. "You know where to find me." He got up and left the office without even touching his tea.

4

"You're not rummaging around for chocolate bars now, are you?" asked Sebastian Hasenkrug as David Büttner rummaged around in the drawer of his desk as soon as Eiko Harms was out the door. "May I remind you that you banned them from the office months ago?"

"Nah, not all of them," Büttner muttered as his arm sank further and further into the depths of the drawer. "I've got the ones all the way back there …"

"*Them?*" Hasenkrug raised his brows disapprovingly. "They have several candy bars stashed away, although …"

"Don't act like my mother for once!" growled Büttner. Grunting contentedly, he immediately pulled his arm out again and beamed at the chocolate bar lying in his hand as joyfully as a long-dead friend. "Wasn't so easy to hide them so Mrs Weniger wouldn't find them." He nodded with satisfaction, then tore the wrapper from the bar and bit into it heartily. "Phew, that feels good!"

"Hm." Hasenkrug looked at him disapprovingly. "And I thought you had long since been cured of this addiction."

"I have," Büttner claimed. "But what am I supposed to do when Jette just …"

"Just cut the bullshit, boss! You're acting as if your daughter is going to war."

"That's how it feels," Büttner mumbled. "You have no idea, Hasenkrug, how much that makes you feel as a father …"

"Jette isn't even on the plane yet, and you …"

Büttner looked at him hopefully. "Do you think she'll change her mind?"

Hasenkrug rolled his eyes. "I should hope not. So, now I suggest we take a closer look at the victim." He turned his screen so that Büttner could also see him.

The photo showing Gina Gloger in her relationship with Eiko Harms was placed next to the one she had taken with her new boyfriend in front of the mirror. "It seems to me that we are dealing with two completely different people," Hasenkrug noted. "The new Gina didn't seem to have too much in common with the old Gina, except that she was in one and the same body."

"What else do we know about her?" inquired Büttner. He bit off another piece of the chocolate bar and then took a sip of coffee. "Parental home, school-leaving qualifications, education, hobbies …" he said after the sticky mass of the bar had mixed with the coffee and he had swallowed it down. How much he had missed this pleasure!

"Gina Gloger, nineteen years old, living in Greetsiel," Hasenkrug repeated what they already knew. "She graduated from the Gymnasium in Norden in the summer with an average of 1.7 and started her studies at the Emden/Leer University of Applied Sciences in the winter semester."

"Oh?" Büttner wondered what this apparently quite intelligent young woman had wanted with the rather plain Eiko Harms. Whether the difference in educational status had also been a reason for the separation? "What did she study?"

"Mechanical Engineering and Design."

Büttner whistled through his teeth. "And this Josef Müller?"

"If you're talking about Jesko Mudder, he graduated from Secondary School and then trained as a car mechanic. He has been working in a garage in Emden for five years."

"One wonders how that fits together," Büttner pondered aloud, without addressing Hasenkrug's point. "And in both cases. Neither our young colleague nor this Mudder seem to be Gina's match."

"At least not as far as their educational status is concerned," Hasenkrug agreed with him. "But we don't know much more about the two men."

"So Jesko Mudder has no criminal record?"

"No, he is as clean as a whistle. Just like Eiko Harms'. But otherwise, the latter would hardly be in the police service."

"Did Gina have any hobbies? She might have been socialising with people that we haven't seen before?"

"She went riding regularly and also had lessons. That was probably one of the reasons why she decided to study in Emden. Not only because of her own horse, which is there, but also because of all the friendships she made at the riding school. That's what I found out from Eiko Harms before you came into the office."

The door opened and Dr Anja Wilkens entered. The forensic pathologist looked completely dishevelled, strands of her long dark hair stuck to her cheeks and forehead. She held a towel in her hands with which she wiped her rain-soaked face. "What weather," she moaned. "The walk from the car park to the police station was enough to make me completely soaked. Thank God Mrs Weniger had a towel ready at once." She looked regretfully at her trainers, which squeaked with every step she took. "I could swear that they assured me in the shop that they were waterproof."

"Presumably they hadn't expected a deluge there either," Büttner grumbled, glancing at the window against which the rain was incessantly slapping. A fresh wind was driving the masses of water almost horizontally in front of them. So far, it had not even become light outside, and it was to be feared that it would stay that way for the rest of the day.

"Is Jette already on the plane?" inquired Anja Wilkens. She gratefully accepted a steaming cup of coffee that Ms Weniger handed to her.

"Wrong topic," muttered Hasenkrug.

"How do you know about that?" asked Büttner after a punishing glance at his assistant.

"I spoke to Susanne on the phone earlier."

"Oh, really? What was there to talk about?"

"Women's stuff."

"Hm." Büttner cleared his throat. "But to answer your question: No, Jette is still on the train to Frankfurt. And I very much hope it stays that way." He looked at the window again. "They can't possibly let a plane take off in this weather."

"Jette will be glad that it looks quite different in Frankfurt," Hasenkrug replied with a grin. "Slightly cloudy, hardly any wind. The deluge is obviously happening exclusively for us."

"Which doesn't surprise me," growled Büttner. "Surely there are no people on earth who can act less godly than the murderous East Frisians."

"Which brings us to the topic." Anja Wilkens handed Hasenkrug a USB stick. "Can you play the files from the folder 'Gina Gloger' onto one of your computer screens?"

"We have much better." Hasenkrug pointed gleefully at a huge monitor mounted on the wall at the other end of the room. "Look what was suddenly on the wall two days ago."

"Oh, new? What did you do to earn it?"

"Clarification of a creeping genocide against the East Frisians," Büttner answered dryly.

"A kind of non-monetary gratuity, then. Congratulations. I didn't know you had such a reward system."

"Neither did I," Büttner replied. "That's why I rather suspect that it's the screen I requested when I took up my duties in this commissariat."

"But it looks quite modern for that."

"Which is probably exclusively due to the fact that the model applied for at the time has long since reached museum maturity," Hasenkrug flattened. He plugged the stick into one of the ports provided for this purpose, whereupon a picture of Gina's battered corpse appeared on the screen. She had little in common with the pretty young woman in the photos.

"For what do you actually honour us with your visit?", Büttner inquired of the forensic pathologist. "Is there something you want to teach us gently?"

"No." Anja Wilkens tapped her cup. "Mrs Weniger told

me on the phone about your new coffee machine. So I thought I'd check if the coffee tastes better than before."

"Well?"

"Equivalent, I would say. Did you also request the coffee machine when you came on duty?"

"Nah." Büttner winked at her. "That was my predecessor."

The doctor laughed, then became serious again and pointed to the screen. "Gina Gloger had drowned."

"So the assumption you made yesterday has been confirmed."

"Not quite."

Büttner raised his eyebrows questioningly.

"I had naturally assumed that she had drowned in the harbour basin."

"She hadn't?"

"No." Anja Wilkens shook her head. "I would rather guess a bathtub."

"Huh?" Büttner looked for signs that she was joking, but she didn't make a face.

"You heard me right, David. Gina drowned in the bathtub, in one filled with bubble bath."

"But she was fully clothed."

"Yes. I assume that was done to deceive us. Or else she was sitting in the bathtub fully clothed. But why would she do that? Presumably the perpetrator was naïve enough to believe that we wouldn't find out if he dumped her body in the harbour basin. Maybe he even hoped that you would classify it as an accident."

"However, that would be more than naïve," Hasenkrug said. "A post-mortem would have taken place in any case."

Anja Wilkens shrugged. "Nowhere is it written that a murderer has to be blessed with a high IQ."

Büttner nodded. He had already arrested so many murderers and manslayers from the most diverse social classes in his life that he had long since stopped believing in differentiated behaviour according to social status.

"She has haematomas all over her body," Anja Wilkens continued. "But especially on her arms and shoulders. For the most part, they were inflicted on her before she died. Some haematomas indicate that she had struggled when her head was forcibly pushed under water, and with a fairly high probability with her bare hands. She was lying on her back when they did this, by the way." She flickered a few close-ups of the injuries across the screen, one after the other, at the press of a button. "Several abrasions and the face smashed almost beyond recognition," she showed more pictures, "are, however, due to the harbour basin, or rather the cutter, on which she was caught. Just like the broken bones. I assume that before her body became entangled with the cutter, it was smashed hard against the harbour wall or similar massive structures in the harbour basin a few times. It was stormy, the water movements even in the harbour correspondingly violent."

"You say she fought back," Hasenkrug said. "How exactly do we have to imagine that?"

"She tried to pull herself free, which she clearly did not succeed in doing. Based on the injuries, I assume that the force was exerted exclusively from outside the tub."

Büttner looked at her questioningly. "By a single person, or could there have been several people involved?"

"Let's put it this way: I don't want to explicitly exclude any of these possibilities. Especially since the body had to be transported somehow to the harbour and into the dock. Gina didn't weigh sixty kilos – so a strong man should be able to do it – but it would be a challenge for a single person. Unfortunately, her body is so torn up in places that I can't say for sure how the killing took place."

"That it was a homicide is certain, though?"

"Yes. It was definitely not a natural death or suicide. There's too much to say it wasn't."

"Could it have been a sex crime?"

"There are no traces of sperm or injuries typical of a rape. So the act probably did not serve to cover up a sexual offence, but followed a different motive."

"Anything else conspicuous?" Büttner wanted to know after he had tried to digest this unpleasant information in a few moments of silence. "Drugs, alcohol?"

"No, neither of those things."

"How long do you think she was in the dock?"

"I can't say exactly, but I assume that she was taken there the night before. It must have been about twelve to seventeen hours before the fire brigade fished her out of the water."

Büttner calculated. "So between midnight and five in the morning?"

"Yes, that should work. She was murdered before that, though. Roughly the day before last, between twenty pm and twenty-two pm. She showed a few more less appetising pictures. "Based on the contents of her stomach, I'm assuming she had eaten dinner shortly before she died."

"What was it?"

"The classic: spaghetti bolognese and salad. She ate the meal not long before she died, it was barely digested."

"First dinner, then full bath, then dock," Hasenkrug summarised. "Any DNA?"

"No, she was in the water too long for that. Of course, it's quite possible that there's some at the crime scene, but we'd have to know it first." She sighed. "Only one thing is certain, unfortunately."

"And that would be?"

"Gina was three months pregnant."

5

The images they saw on the internet could be described as offensive, but they remained largely what was commonly called adult. Nevertheless, Büttner found it disconcerting to see them in the unusually large format that the new screen gave.

"It's quite possible that one or the other didn't like the way Gina presented herself," remarked Mark Humboldt. The head of forensics had come to Büttner and Hasenkrug's office to present them with the findings of the social media research. "But it's hard to believe that someone would be so freewheeling as to knit a murder motive out of it." He clicked through a few more pictures, most of them showing Gina and Jesko as a happy as well as erotic couple.

"Was there a social media shitstorm in response to these pictures?" asked Hasenkrug.

"All in all, the comments on Instagram, Facebook and co. are benevolent to …" Humboldt grimaced, "well, frivolous. Men in particular have commented in a less than respectful manner, but that's hardly surprising. It's not uncommon that guys like Jesko Mudder are celebrated like heroes by uptight guys who act like Rambo in the anonymity of the internet."

"Nevertheless, it cannot be ruled out that someone felt

put on the spot by these pictures," Büttner gave as an indication.

Humboldt shrugged his shoulders. "That's the way it is on the net. There are plenty of moralisers there, just like some feminists who think Gina's performance is a betrayal of the women's movement. On the other hand, there are also those who basically find everything cool that drives the former up the wall. If you read the comments, you get the feeling that you're in the middle of a war. Everything is sharpening knives, whether in one direction or the other. Only respectful or even appreciative cooperation is sought in vain."

"Whatever," growled Büttner. "Have you found anything in all this clutter that at least makes ours sit up and take notice?"

"You're talking about a specific threat of violence or murder?"

"For example."

Humboldt continued to click through Gina's Instagram account. "There's a lady here who's had her sights set on Gina for a good four months. Julia Vogler. I quote: *you're dead if I catch you, bitch. Since when does Jesko like zombies? Get the fuck out of Jesko's life, you victim, or I'll see to your exit myself.*"

Büttner screwed up his face. "Charming. And she writes all that in public?"

"Yup. For everyone to read."

The profile picture of a young woman appeared on the screen, who must have been about the victim's age. Just like Gina, she was extremely pretty, albeit in a completely different way. Whereas Gina's photos showed her with a northern German cool charm, Julia's dark curly hair presented her as a fiery southern beauty. "We then took a look at Julia's profile."

"Well?"

Humboldt lifted his empty cup. "First another coffee from the fantastic new machine, then I'll give you what you want."

Büttner refrained from commenting on this, but just pointed silently to the door.

"If you're going, bring me one too," Hasenkrug urged his colleague.

"I'd really like to know what attracts people, especially young people, to these supposedly social platforms," Büttner pondered aloud. His fingers itched to reach for another chocolate bar, but he forced himself to abstain. After his heart attack, his cardiologist showed himself to be reasonably satisfied with him for the first time, so it would be more than unreasonable to fall back into unhealthy patterns of behaviour. Besides, he didn't set much store by being caught snacking by Mrs Weniger and having to confess to having deceived her with an iron reserve of chocolate bars.

"They are vying for recognition," Hasenkrug said.

Büttner looked irritated. "I'm courting recognition? But I don't have anything …"

"The young people on the social platforms. *They are* vying for recognition."

Büttner snorted. "If they didn't stand half naked in front of the mirror but got involved in Youth programmes, for example, we'd all have more of it." He looked at his assistant frowning. "What are you grinning at now?"

"I don't think young people are concerned with social recognition. It's more the opposite.

"And that would be?"

"Provocation."

Mark Humboldt came back. He pressed a steaming mug into Hasenkrug's hand, then turned his attention back to his laptop. "I'm quite envious of your new monitor, by the way," he said as another image appeared. "Applied for one of those years ago. Then when you consider that the coffee machine is new too …" He sighed. "Just the other day I said to my wife that even in socialism the Trabbis were out the door faster than they let us participate in technical progress in a Federal German authority."

"Are you done whining?" asked Büttner. "Then we could get back to our work."

"Not everyone can go through life as relaxed as you, boss," Hasenkrug grinned. "Speaking of which, is Jette already on the plane to Cape Town?"

Humboldt's head flew around. "Jette is flying to Cape Town?"

"Yes. And she is staying for several months." Büttner's voice dripped with self-pity, but he did not meet with the hoped-for response from Humboldt either. Humboldt's eyes widened and he exclaimed: "Several months in Cape Town? Wow, I've always dreamed of that! What a lucky girl!" He looked pleadingly at Büttner. "Can you adopt me, David?"

"Haha, what a laugh we had." Büttner snorted disparagingly. "What was it like with this Jutta …"

"Julia Vogler," corrected Hasenkrug.

Humboldt cleared his throat. "Whatever." He called up

another Instagram account, and only seconds later a couple of pictures appeared showing a young couple, who were strikingly similar to those of Gina.

"So Julia was also involved with Jesko Mudder," Hasenkrug noted. "Seems to be his scam to degrade the young women to sex objects in front of the camera."

"Too bad they don't seem to notice or seem to think it's just as cool," Humboldt interjected. "If you ask me, they both don't look too unhappy. And from the reaction to Gina's posts, I think it's safe to conclude that Julia would be only too happy to take her ex-boyfriend back."

"When are the pictures from?"

"They're about ten months old." Humboldt reached for his smartphone as it announced a message. "Guys, buckle up!" Only a little later, a video sequence appeared on the screen. It, too, showed Julia and Jesko, though what one got to see was now clearly pornographic.

"Okay, that's enough." Büttner made a sign to his colleague to stop the film. He had seen enough.

"Did you crack Julia's private site?" asked Hasenkrug.

"Nah. Quite the opposite. Our IT specialist found a website where you can see such films. For money, of course. Run by Jesko Mudder."

"That means there are other women there at the … uh…"

"Sex?", Hasenkrug helped out.

"Yes. Or whatever they're up to. So, there are other women with Jesko Mudder to be seen on the website?", Büttner inquired.

"Yes, and not just a few. I'd say the guy has created a lucrative and entertaining sideline for himself."

"Do the women know about this?"

"I don't know. It's your job to find out."

"Is there such a film with Gina too?"

"No. Not so far. At least none have been uploaded yet. Which is not to say none exist. We'd have to sift through Mudder's technical equipment for that." Humboldt looked from one to the other. "That's why we've been trying to find out where Jesko Mudder, or rather his smartphone is at the moment. Without success."

"He turned it off?"

"Looks like it. It hasn't been logged in anywhere since the night before last."

"Do you have an exact time?", Hasenkrug wanted to know.

"Twenty-one eighteen. From then on, his mobile phone has been dead."

"That matches Anja's information on the approximate time of Gina Gloger's death. And where was the mobile phone last logged on?"

"In Greetsiel. Not far from the Gloger family home. Maybe even in it."

"You're talking about the house where Gina also lived?", Büttner made sure.

"She lives in a granny flat in her parents' house, yes."

"And Jesko Mudder? Where does he live?"

"He has a flat in Emden. At the new market."

"Is he staying there right now?"

"I don't know. Your job."

"And you found all that out this morning?" Büttner nodded appreciatively. "You guys are really on your toes."

Humboldt indicated a bow. "Thank you for the flowers, David. But thanks to social media, it's not too hard to get information these days. They are the diary of the young generation, so to speak. It's frightening what information many people feel they have to share with the rest of the world. Voluntarily, mind you. And not just about themselves, but about others as well."

"Gina Gloger was pregnant, as Anja informed us," Hasenkrug said. "I assume there is no difficulty in finding out who the child's father is?"

"If we can get a comparison DNA, then this should be one of our easiest exercises."

"Okay." Büttner patted his thighs and stood up. "Then I'll take care of search warrants for Gina's flat and for Jesko's." He nodded at Hasenkrug. "I want the searches to take place at the same time. So let Chris Bäumler know that he will have to provide us with two teams at short notice."

"Will do, boss." Hasenkrug reached for the phone.

"Okay, I'll get back to work then," Humboldt said. He looked at his empty cup. "I'm sure Mrs Weniger will give me another coffee, or what do you think?"

Büttner left this question in the room because he certainly had more important things to do now than worry about the forensic scientist's coffee. He nodded to Humboldt and immediately picked up the phone to ask the judge for the search warrants.

6

David Büttner only had the search warrant for Gina's granny flat with him pro forma. Experience had shown that the relatives did not object to a search of the victim's living quarters even without such a document, since it was usually in their interest to convict the perpetrator. However, if Gina's parents objected, they could always do it this way.

"They have not only lost their daughter, but also their grandchild," said Sebastian Hasenkrug as they walked towards the Glogers' house in pouring rain. "We have to consider the possibility that they didn't know about the pregnancy."

"Yes, we have to." In the meantime, Büttner had heard from colleagues that Gina's parents were apparently in a state of grief. Allegedly, her mother had even threatened to take her own life in order to follow her daughter into the afterlife. And even if, in the opinion of the police psychologist, this had simply been said in the first moments of pain, it was not a good starting point for the upcoming conversation. Especially not when the parents also learned about the death of their unborn grandchild. What would their reaction be? The most diverse scenarios were conceivable. Büttner had given up worrying about it, because most of the time things turned out quite differently than he had feared or hoped. The only fact was that this was not a visit for which he liked to be in the front row.

The Glogers lived in the old centre of Greetsiel in a modern two-storey, cubically built house made of white clinker brick and with large windows. It had obviously been built in the garden of an existing property, because right next door was an older farm worker's house, without a fence separating the two. The latter was one of the traditional Frisian houses with mullioned windows that were still numerous in Greetsiel. The newer building, on the other hand, satisfied the other, above all more ostentatious demands. The open space around the two houses was enough for a generously laid-out garden with bushes, trees and herbaceous borders, all of which looked rather desolate at this time of year.

When Hasenkrug rang the doorbell, it took a while before anything happened. But then the door was opened. A well-dressed, carefully coiffed and made-up woman of perhaps fifty stood before them. Her blond hair was tied back in a braid. She looked serious, but there was nothing to suggest that she had been crying. "Yes, please?"

"Moin." Büttner introduced himself and Hasenkrug. "You are Mrs Gloger?"

"No. I'm Wiebke Storm, a friend of Amke's. Please come in." She took a step back to let them pass. "You're late," she then stated, not without reproach in her voice. "We were expecting you yesterday."

"It's due to the circumstances," Büttner replied. "As we were told, the parents of the victim … that is, the Glogers, were visited by a counsellor yesterday. We didn't want to disturb them." He looked around the spacious hallway, lined with shiny black tiles, from which several glass doors led off and, moreover, a curved staircase led up to the upper floor. With its two cosy-looking leather armchairs, two large antique display cabinets and an ancient-looking sailor's chest, this room looked more like a living room than a hallway.

The living space was correspondingly impressive. Selected furniture, valuable-looking decorations, paintings and statues by contemporary artists. The huge living area merged seamlessly into a kitchen in glossy black, with a fire crackling in the large fireplace in the middle of the room.

Büttner didn't know what he had expected, but this certainly wasn't it. None of what he saw here was in keeping with the cliché that he, at least, had previously associated with a Greetsiel crab-fishing family. It seemed to him that the cottage, which he now discovered – just like the Greetsiel twin mills – when looking out of one of the floor-to-ceiling panorama windows, was much more in keeping with a fishing family.

"Commissioners Büttner and Hasenpflug are from the criminal investigation department," Wiebke Storm said, addressing two people whom Büttner assumed were Gina's parents and who looked at them from infinitely sad eyes. They sat huddled close together in one of the two massive sofas that dominated the middle of the living room, separated by a solid wooden table.

"Krug. My name is Hasenkrug," Hasenkrug hurried to say.

"You're late," the man said after nodding curtly and powerlessly at Hasenkrug's objection. It sounded more resigned than reproachful. He seemed to be a handsome man, even though he sat hunched up and thus appeared smaller than he actually was. With his jeans, checked flannel shirt and calloused hands, he didn't quite want to fit into these swanky surroundings. Neither did his wife, who was not at all smartly dressed, as would have been expected in view of the wealth on display, but wore a washed-out beige sweatshirt with jeans. At their feet lay a medium-sized, fluffy dog, which Büttner had initially mistaken for a pillow. Now, however, the dog lifted its head and looked at him no less sadly than its master and mistress. He seemed to feel the sadness. No sooner had he looked up than he buried his head between his paws again.

Büttner explained the reason for their late arrival, which was acknowledged by both with a nod. "The counsellor helped us a lot," sniffled Gina's mother, who Büttner knew was called Amke Gloger. Then she broke into a heart-rending sob and buried her head in the crook of her husband's neck.

"Why is someone doing this to us and our child?" the man asked with a helpless look at Büttner, as if he could give him an answer.

"We … er… are here to find out exactly that," Büttner answered evasively. "Do you see yourself in a position to answer a few questions? We would also like to take a look at your daughter's rooms. As we were told, she lived here in a granny flat?"

"Yes."

Büttner took this as an answer to both questions.

"Please, sit down," Wiebke Storm spoke up. "I'll make some tea then. Or would you prefer coffee?"

"Tea is quite wonderful," Büttner replied. "Thank you." He lowered himself into the sofa opposite the couple, which turned out to be surprisingly comfortable. Hasenkrug followed his example.

"Our children thought we should furnish the house in a modern way," said Tjark Gloger, as Büttner silently let his gaze wander around the room to give the couple a chance to collect themselves. "So we left the decorating to them. But we don't really like it that much." He wrapped his arms even tighter around his wife as she began to tremble. "I keep saying to my wife that we'd better move to the little house I grew up in. Those were happy days and it suits us much better. So now that my parents are gone and the little house is empty …" He let the rest of the sentence hang unspoken in the air.

"Gina thinks it's great," his wife added in a voice as thin as parchment. She smiled sadly at her husband. "Remember how proud she was when she carried us out here? Just like her brothers and sisters. We didn't dare say we didn't really like it."

"We were on holiday when they decorated it with the help of an interior designer," her husband added explanatorily. "It was supposed to be a surprise." He laughed unhappily. "Well, and it was."

"Do your other children also live here in the house?" Büttner asked. He was deeply touched by this couple. They must have loved their children very much if they were so willing to accept their wishes. But what did it say about the children that they planned so far ahead of their parents' tastes? Either they were extremely naïve – or simply interested in the status that needed to be shown to the outside world. And why on earth were they not here to stand by their parents in this difficult hour?

"No. Keno lives in Bremen and Luisa in Weener," Amke Gloger explained. "They both have families already. Gina is … was our youngest. Our … nestling." The last words were little more than a whisper. "Our big ones went on holiday together, to Thailand," she added, as if she had read Büttner's mind. "Now, of all times. They're trying to get a flight home, but it's not so easy, because they are six people, after all. Luisa was crying so much on the phone and there was nothing I could do. But the others will comfort her, don't you think?"

Her pleading look hit Büttner right in the heart. Here was clearly a mother sitting in front of them who, regardless of her own condition, would do anything for her children. And now one of her chicks had been brutally taken from her. What had fate been thinking? "Of course they will," he replied with a smile. "That's what family is for, isn't it?"

Amke Gloger smiled back gratefully. "You're telling me, Commissioner."

The doorbell rang and the Glogers looked up questioningly. "I don't want any visitors now," said the woman. "I can't take it at the moment."

Her husband patted her hand. "Wiebke knows about it, she won't let anyone in.

"I assume it's our colleagues from the forensics department," Büttner said. "Would it be possible for them to … Gina's rooms?"

"Oh, yes of course."

"It may be that we take a few things with us to …"

"Whatever you need. The main thing is that you find the monster who did this to us," growled Gloger.

"Okay. Thank you." When Wiebke Storm immediately reported the arrival of Chris Bäumler and his colleagues, Büttner gave his assistant a hint to take care of the forensics team.

"When did you last see your daughter?" asked Büttner after Hasenkrug had left the room and Wiebke Storm had provided them with tea and biscuits and sat down with them. When she poured the tea, the crackling of the sugar cubes, which did not fit in at all with the cool atmosphere of this house, irritated him for a brief moment. Generally, he always associated drinking tea with cosiness. A feeling that corresponded neither to the situation nor to the sterility of this house. Nevertheless, it did him good to have something warming to drink, as he noted with satisfaction after the first sip.

"That was two days ago," Tjark Gloger answered. "Gina left the house in the afternoon." Tears came to his eyes, which he bashfully wiped away. But his despair broke through nonetheless when he said in a tear-choked voice: "We argued. I … I told her to go to hell." He shouted out the next few sentences: "Surely that's not acceptable, Commissioner! It can't be possible that the last thing I said to my little girl was that she should go to hell! How am I ever supposed to make up for that?!"

Phew! Büttner was deeply moved by this pain and swallowed hard a few times. Sometimes it was anything but easy to keep a professional distance.

"But she knows you love her," Amke Gloger tried to comfort her husband. "She knows she's daddy's little girl." Tears ran down her cheek again, too, and she mechanically accepted the handkerchief Wiebke Storm handed her. It seemed as routine as the long-rehearsed scene of a play.

But unfortunately it was not that, but the bitter reality.

"What was the argument about that you had with Gina?" asked Büttner, even though he felt anything but comfortable continuing to poke at the wound.

Gloger blew his nose loudly into his handkerchief, then said: "Of course about that good-for-nothing she's been hanging around with lately."

"Does this no-good have a name?"

"Jesko. Jesko Mudder." Gloger extended his index finger in Büttner's direction. "You can arrest him right now. I know it was him."

"That he was what?", Büttner inquired, although he was sure he knew.

"That it was him who … who … who … Gina." His voice failed him.

"He thinks it was Jesko who killed Gina," his wife finished the statement. "Which wouldn't surprise me either, because Jesko has always messed things up." She then gave her friend a meaningful look, whereupon she nodded, as if she too could not imagine that anyone other than Jesko could be considered for a murder.

"And why do you think that?"

"Well …" Again her gaze brushed her friend, who pressed her lips together, "because he didn't want the child after all."

This came as such a surprise that Büttner almost choked on his tea. He had been sure that Gina's pregnancy had been a secret well-kept by her. "You knew that Gina was pregnant?"

The Glogers looked at him with wide eyes. "Of course. She was our child after all. But how do you know that?"

"It's in the post-mortem report."

"So. Then … it's true."

"You had doubts?"

Amke Gloger dabbed at her eyes with another handkerchief her friend handed her. "Oh, you know, Commissioner … Gina had changed so much recently. Honestly, we didn't even know what was true and what wasn't anymore. We … we hardly recognised her since she started hanging out with Jesko."

"I always told her to stay with Eiko," Gloger said. "He's a decent fellow, I said. But she didn't want to hear that. Instead, it absolutely had to be that good-for-nothing Jesko. She didn't listen to me when I said to her that he was only after one thing and that he was taking advantage of her. After all, it's known all over East Frisia what a hooligan he is."

"And now she had let him loose her child too," his wife added, sniffling. "I can't say I was thrilled about it, but … but …" She gave an exasperated sob. "But it was Gina's child, our grandchild! No one has the right to just … the two of them!" She threw her hands in the air. "No one has the right, do you understand?!"

"And you are sure that Jesko knew about the pregnancy?" asked Büttner.

"Gina said for sure. And that he's happy. But I don't believe it."

"But instead you believe that Jesko Mudder killed your daughter because she was pregnant by him," Büttner summarised. "Did I understand that correctly?"

"Yes. Why else do you think he disappeared off the face of the earth?! He would have come here long ago, or at least he would be at home if he hadn't."

"How do you know he's not at home?"

Gloger snorted and raised his clenched fist in the air. "You don't think that the people of Greetsiel are going to put up with that from someone who had just walked in and taken our girl and our grandchild. They went to see, of course. He's lucky he wasn't at home, otherwise …" He gestured a cut in the throat with his hands.

Oh dear, that didn't sound good! Büttner thought of the riot they had witnessed last night at Greetsiel harbour. Could it have had something to do with the call for vigilante justice?

"Do you know about the fight last night at the harbour?" he addressed the question to Gina's parents.

"Yeah, sure, Wiebke said something about it."

"Was that about Gina?"

"Yes. And nope."

Büttner raised his eyebrows questioningly.

"Yes, because that fueled the mood when she was found," Gloger explained. "And no, because they are always clashing lately."

"Who are they and why are they clashing?"

"Our fishermen. They're always fighting with the Dutch. It's a hard time for us crab fishermen, you know. And the Dutch don't do any better."

Büttner had read about the dispute between the German and Dutch crab fishermen over fishing grounds and fishing rights in the newspaper, but he didn't want to go into the subject at this point. "So, the dispute was not primarily about Gina?"

"Nah. But I'm telling you, that's what fueled the mood."

Büttner's smartphone announced a message. "Please excuse me for a moment." He fished it out of his trouser pocket. The second forensics team was at Jesko Mudder's flat. They had gained entry with the help of the caretaker, but had not found the young man. His electronic devices had also disappeared, only a few cables left behind were hanging from the wall.

Büttner stood up. "Please excuse me, I have to make a phone call." He left the room and dialled his secretary's number. "Please arrange for a public search for Jesko Mudder. The full programme. He seems to have disappeared. We are looking for him as a witness. If he does not respond to the APB, he will make himself our prime suspect. I hope he is aware of that."

"Or he doesn't get in touch because he's dead too," Mrs Weniger indicated.

"Let's hope not."

"How are things with the Glogers?"

Büttner sighed. "They are parents who have lost their child. How is it supposed to be there?"

"I see."

Büttner hung up and went back into the living room.

"Is there anything new?" asked Tjark Gloger.

Büttner passed over this question. "What do you know about Jesko Mudder?" he continued the interrupted conversation.

"That I would rather see him dead than alive," was Gloger's unequivocal answer.

"But Tjark, you mustn't say things like that!"

"What?" he hissed at his wife. "That pig has our daughter on his conscience. So I say what I think, it's that simple. He can only hope the police find him before I do."

"Mr Gloger, I understand that you …"

"You don't understand shit, Commissioner! Do you have a daughter?"

"Yes, but …"

"Then I'd like to see you when someone does to your daughter what was done to our Gina!"

"Tjark, please," his wife whined. "The inspector only wants to help us. And remember your blood pressure! Not that you too could …" She burst into tears again.

Büttner decided it was time to retire. There was only one question he wanted to get off his chest. "Had Gina decided to keep the child?"

"Yes," Amke Gloger said quietly. "She wanted it badly. That's what the argument was about, wasn't it, that Gina and my husband …" She fell silent.

"This child would have ruined her whole life," Gloger growled. "She had only just started studying and … well, what's the use of it all now." There was a deep sadness in his eyes as he added with a bitter laugh: "You shouldn't believe the things you think about when there's actually no problem. Because let's be honest: since when are children a problem? If you were to ask me today, Commissioner, Gina could bring in a dozen children from that good-for-nothing, and I would change all of them myself. But in life you almost never realise what's really important as long as everything is going well. And suddenly it's too late."

Büttner drank his tea, then stood up. "I'll be on my way, but first I'll stop by to see my colleagues upstairs. So, if you have any questions or want to tell me something …"

The Glogers showed no reaction. They were apparently so absorbed in their pain that they no longer paid any attention to him. He nodded to Wiebke Storm, who nodded back, barely noticeable.

7

"No laptop, no mobile phone, nothing," muttered David Büttner when Sebastian Hasenkrug and he later were sitting in the car on the way back to Emden to take a closer look at Jesko Mudder's ex-girlfriend Julia Vogler. "Then Gina might have taken the devices to Mudder's place …"

"… from where they also disappeared, however, as we know from Chris Bäumler," Hasenkrug completed the sentence. "That doesn't make things any easier, of course. But at least Gina shared her life with the rest of the world on social media. It's a lot of work for the forensic colleagues to sort through all that, but they have to get through it."

"The biggest headache for me is where Jesko Mudder is hiding," Büttner replied. "Let's hope that our search will be successful. But it's possible that the guy has already gone abroad, and then it gets complicated."

"Do you really think Mudder killed his girlfriend because she was expecting his child?"

"It wouldn't be the first time something like this has happened."

"Nah. But somehow …" Hasenkrug frowned. "He could have had that easier than drowning her in the bathtub."

Büttner raised his index finger. "In his own bathtub, mind you! The traces seem clear, as the Spusi team told us.

So why shouldn't it be the bathtub when the opportunity arises?"

"And on top of that, there just happens to be a second person around who also thinks murdering a pregnant woman is a cool idea?" Hasenkrug shook his head. "Nah, something doesn't add up there."

"But it is possible that the pregnancy was not the motive for the murder," Büttner said. "It's possible that Gina found out that Mudder was using his porn site to feed young women to drooling men and threatened to turn him in."

"She had just decided to have the child together," Hasenkrug replied. "Surely she would have felt differently about it if she had known about the porn site. Between the argument with her father after she left the house in a rage and her death, she would only have had a few hours to find out about it. Is that realistic?"

"We still don't even know for sure that Jesko Mudder is the father of the child. If he is not, we would theoretically have a new motive for murder. And so on, and so on. As long as we don't have any certain facts, we shouldn't lose ourselves in quibbles. Let the forensics do their work and then we'll see."

Büttner pulled out his smartphone. "Oh, a message from Jette."

"What does she write? Is she already on the plane?"

Büttner sighed. "May I give you some advice, Hasenkrug?"

"Only if it can't be avoided."

"Don't under any circumstances become a police investigator when you grow up. Your logical thinking won't allow it." Büttner tapped his wristwatch. "Jette took the train to

Frankfurt this morning. So how could she already be on the plane now, with all the fuss you have to go through at the airport? Not to mention the Deutsche Bahn, which likes to get lost in the middle of nowhere, far from any timetable."

"Thanks for the tutoring. And what does she write now?"

"She has arrived at the airport and is queuing at check-in."

"That sounds promising for a start."

Büttner grimaced. "If you say so. Oh. She's sending some pictures too." He opened the pictures and heaved another sigh. "They're photos of Debbie that she sent her from Cape Town."

"What kind of photos?"

"Beach, sea, mountains, flowers, sunset, Debbie," Büttner enumerated.

Hasenkrug parked at the side of the road, having reached their destination. "Let me see it!" He made a prompting gesture and accepted the mobile phone. "Oh, wow! That's …! Shit, it's nice there!"

"Get a grip on yourself, Hasenkrug!" Büttner remarked sourly. "You really don't have to travel to Cape Town to have a good time. After all, we also live where other people go on holiday."

Hasenkrug looked at him pityingly. "Really now, boss? You're comparing East Frisia to Cape Town?"

"Hm." Büttner took the mobile phone from him and pocketed it again.

"Who is this Debbie, anyway? She looks sympathetic."

"Jette's English teacher. And also, her landlady. I'd like to see her police record."

Hasenkrug sighed, "Sorry, boss, but you really can't be helped. Just be happy that Jette has done so well. You should be proud of her. Not everyone dares such an adventure."

"Use the word adventure again, Hasenkrug, and I'll have you transferred to Timbuktu!"

Hasenkrug undid his belt. "If you ask me, boss, Jette could have had it worse in life. Now just imagine if she had become a boring sausage like her father."

Büttner decided he didn't want to have this discussion anymore and would rather concentrate on the case again. So, without another word, he opened the car door and got out.

They headed for the apartment building where Julia Vogler lived. Before they even pressed the bell button, the front door opened and an elderly gentleman with a cigarette in his mouth and a dog that looked even older stepped out. They both screwed up their faces in disgust at the rain pelting the pavement. The dog stopped by Büttner and sniffed his trousers.

"Do you have a dog too?" the man croaked in a smoker's raspy voice as he tried to open his umbrella, which proved bulky. Meanwhile, his cigarette was hit several times by raindrops and finally went out.

"Yes. Heinrich."

"See, I thought so." He dropped his soggy cigarette to the ground. "My Renate can smell males a mile off. Old as she is, she still wants to be mated. Women! The older the better, I always say."

That was more information than Büttner needed. Nor could he imagine that Heinrich would have taken a liking to this shaggy lady.

"Do you want to go in there?" the man croaked.

"That's the reason I'm holding the door open," Hasenkrug said.

"Who do you want to see?"

"Can you tell us on which floor Julia Vogler lives?"

As if he had said something naughty, the man eyed them one after the other with a disdainful look, then he pursed his mouth in disgust and said: "I should have guessed that." He padded away with his dog and the no longer quite appropriate umbrella and growled, shaking his head: "But that they now come during the day and then in pairs … ts, Renate, we can't approve of that."

Büttner and Hasenkrug looked at each other and shrugged. Hasenkrug counted off the doorbells. "According to this, Julia Vogler lives on the third floor. Stairs or lift?"

"Are you kidding?" Büttner headed straight for the lift. Hasenkrug grinned broadly – and took the stairs.

When they reached the top, they stood directly in front of the right door, as a name plate told them. Loud hip-hop music could be heard from inside, so it was to be feared that Julia Vogler would not hear the ringing at all. But apparently her hearing was better than average, because the door opened only shortly after the bell rang.

"Hi, guys," they were greeted by a woman chewing gum who pulled one of her wireless headphones out of her ear. Why she was wearing them was beyond Büttner, because after all, the music was blaring to the point of God-awfulness. He eyed the woman. She was dressed in jeans and a baggy shirt. She had twisted her dark curly hair up into a bun and placed it in the middle of her head. Her eyes were made up with black kohl, her mouth with purple lipstick. "Do we have a date?"

Büttner pulled out his service card and held it in front of her face. "My name is Büttner, this is my colleague Hasenkrug. We are from the criminal investigation department."

"Gross." She blew her gum into a bubble and popped it.

"We've come for Gina Gloger."

Julia's forehead clouded over. "Did that bitch report me or what?"

Büttner raised his eyebrows in astonishment. Was she playing a game with them, or was it actually possible that she had not yet heard about Gina's murder? "What reason could Ms Gloger have for reporting you?"

"I don't know." The next bubble of chewing gum burst. She picked up the sticky mass again with her finger and pushed it back into her mouth. "For harassment?" She grinned.

"Did you bother her then?"

A steep crease appeared between her eyes. "What is this going to be? A guessing game? What's up with that bitch?"

She was a gifted actress. Büttner thought it highly unlikely that she, of all people, had not yet known about Gina's death. In the times of social media, where Julia, as they knew by now, was virtually twenty-four hours a day, such a thing was simply inconceivable. Not to mention all the text messages that young people used to bombard each other with.

"You're not seriously telling me that you haven't heard

about Gina's death yet," Hasenkrug said – whereupon Julia stared at him as if he had turned into a zombie before her eyes.

"H-how dead?" Julia seemed so taken aback that she even forgot to chew her gum.

"May we come in?"

"If you have to." She preceded them into a narrow hallway. When they entered, she took two steps back and kicked the decrepit flat door so that it clanged shut.

Immediately afterwards, they entered a room whose walls were only sparsely plastered. On one of the walls was a large spray-painted antifa emblem, otherwise there was no wall decoration. The furniture consisted of a slatted frame with a mattress, a clothes rail, a shelf in which clothes were piled up in no visible order, and a worn armchair that probably came from grandma's days.

"Could you please turn off the music?" roared Büttner against the deafening volume of two speakers.

"Huh?" Julia pretended not to understand and grinned cheekily.

Hasenkrug then took two steps towards an outdated-looking stereo and pressed the off button.

"So, what about Gina now?" Julia furrowed her brow but refrained from responding when the music was turned off. She also seemed to have come to the conclusion that the claim that Gina was dead could not be true, because she said: "Whatever she said about me, it's not true."

"Where were you the last two days?" asked Büttner.

"Why?"

"Just answer my question, please."

"Are you guys going for authoritarian state power here, or what? I know my rights and…"

"Now hold your breath!" Hasenkrug snapped at her. "If it suits you better, we can continue the conversation at the police station. So where have you been for the last two days? A clear answer, please, or you'll find yourself in our interrogation room faster than you can say Antifa!"

Büttner tried to look as unconcerned as possible, although he was just as surprised by his assistant's unusually stern appearance as Julia Vogler apparently was, for she stared open-mouthed at Hasenkrug and seemed to be considering whether the best reaction to this verbal attack was war or peace.

She opted for peace. "All right, if you really want to know: I was in the backwater of Brandenburg for a week. Three more steps and I would have been in Poland."

"Brandenburg." Hasenkrug looked at her incredulously. "To do what?"

"Have my peace." She brushed a curl behind her ear that had come loose from her bun. "I just wanted to have my peace. I rented a houseboat, went out on a lake and that was it."

"Alone?" asked Büttner.

"Would I have had my peace otherwise?"

"Can you prove that?"

"Sure. I rented a houseboat. Do you think that's possible anonymously?" She picked up her smartphone, which she had placed on a side table, tapped and swiped at it and finally showed Hasenkrug the booking confirmation and a few selfies showing her on that very houseboat. "Satisfied?"

"Can you take a screenshot of the confirmation and send it to me? But in such a way that all the important information is on it." Hasenkrug handed her his business card, only a little later his smartphone announced the message. "Thank you."

"Don't mention it." Julia popped another bubble of chewing gum.

"When did you come back?" asked Büttner.

"Exactly two hours ago. Do you also want to see my train ticket?" Without waiting for a reply, she took another screenshot. "I have nothing to hide, no matter what that bitch claims."

"Are you that obtuse or don't you want to understand?" asked Büttner angrily. "Gina Gloger is dead. She can't claim anything anymore."

Julia looked at him with wide eyes. "Really now? You weren't joking?"

"We're homicide detectives. It's a pretty humourless job. Is that enough of an answer for you?"

"M-murder?" Julia took a step back, dropped into the armchair and slapped her hands in front of her face. "Oh fuck!"

"Surely you don't mean to tell me that you didn't know about this?"

"Nah, man. I really didn't."

Hasenkrug snorted. "You're on social media day and night. And you seriously want to tell us that you …"

"I had my phone off, man! The whole week. Digital Detox. Ever heard of it? Yo, man, I wanted my peace, I told you that already!" She made a spacey motion with her arms. "I didn't want anything to do with all this shit, at least for a few days. You can believe me or not. But I did. I just turned my phone back on and was checking the news when you rang."

"Well, it won't be difficult for us to check."

"Do what you want, man." She scowled at Hasenkrug. "Why are you coming to me with this?"

"*You're dead if I catch you, bitch,*" Hasenkrug quoted after glancing at his smartphone. "*Get the fuck out of Jesko's life, you victim, or I'll see to your exit myself.*" Hasenkrug shrugged his shoulders. "And suddenly she has her exit. But of course, it's a bit far-fetched to get any funny ideas about that."

"You have no right to check up on me."

"We don't need to. It's publicly visible on the internet," Hasenkrug countered. "Such threats are punishable by law, by the way. But our colleagues will take care of that. We are only interested in whether you carried out these threats."

Julia extended her index finger in Hasenkrug's direction. "Hey, man, don't pin this on me! I was in Brandenburg, okay? I've got nothing to do with it!" For the first time, a certain uncertainty could be heard in her voice.

"And you also have no idea who else besides you could have felt such a deep hatred for Gina that they would kill her?"

Julia seemed to think about it, but then shook her head. "Nah, man, not a plan. I really don't. I mean, murder is really something."

"Maybe it has something to do with the porn site." Büttner watched Julia's reaction. To all appearances, however, she did not seem to know what he was talking about, because she merely looked at him frowning. "What kind of porn site? Yo, man, how sick does this get?"

Büttner nodded at Hasenkrug, who then called up the video from Jesko Mudder's website and played it before Julia's eyes.

At first, the young woman acted bored. But when she registered that she was watching herself having sex, she turned white as a sheet from one moment to the next. "W-where did you get that?" she asked hoarsely.

"From the internet."

"W-what?" She looked honestly shocked.

It became clear that the young women had no idea that Jesko Mudder was abusing their trust in such a shameful way. And they may not even have known that they were being filmed having sex.

"Did you know that these recordings were being made?" asked Büttner. "Or in other words: Did you consent to the recordings at the time?"

"N-no. I … had no idea." Julia's voice trembled. "And that one …" She made a nervous gesture with her hand, "you can really watch that on the internet?"

"As far as you are willing to pay for it."

Julia shot up from the chair, a dangerous glint in her eyes. "That fucker is peddling our … He's peddling this as a …?" Her voice failed her with indignation.

"As porn, yes." Hasenkrug nodded. "And believe me, Julia, you're not the only one who's been offered to some pervert as a jerk-off."

Julia started pacing up and down the room, running her

hands through her curls again and again. "Fuck, man, this can't be happening! Fuck, fuck, fuck!"

"Do you still want Jesko back now?", Büttner couldn't help asking, but she didn't pay him any attention, instead seemed completely preoccupied with herself.

"Where … where do you find that? So … on which site?"

"Not at all anymore. Hasenkrug explained. "The site has been shut down. Police investigations have been launched against the operator. So you can rest assured."

"Unconcerned, haha, you're really funny." It sounded bitter. "Did …" She swallowed hard. "Did Jesko sell the films, or did he upload them himself?"

"He is the operator of the platform," Hasenkrug said. "In this respect, we can probably assume that he uploaded the films himself."

Julia pinched her lips together and nodded. "Shit, man," she pressed out a few moments later, "I'm sick to my stomach." She slapped her hand over her mouth and ran out the door. Only a little later, a retching sound could be heard, probably from the bathroom.

"You wouldn't happen to know where Jesko Mudder is?" asked Büttner when Julia stumbled back into the room minutes later, visibly shaken.

"He's lucky I don't know," came back miserably, but there was also an undercurrent of anger. She raised her eyes, misty with tears. "Did he … was it Jesko who … Gina? Did he film her too?"

"We don't know," said Büttner. "But if you have any clues in the near future as to where Mudder can be found, please let us know immediately."

Julia was silent, her eyes narrowed to slits.

"Ms…uh…did you hear me?"

"All right, Commissioner," she confirmed in a gloomy voice.

It sounded unconvincing, so to be on the safe side Büttner added: "Whatever revenge plans may be ripening in your head right now: leave it to us to bring him to justice."

"I want to be alone now."

"Do we understand each other, Ms … er… Julia? No going it alone, no vigilante justice! You would only harm yourself with that."

"Didn't you understand?!", Julia shouted at them completely abruptly. "I want to be alone! So, fuck off! You're all sick, you bastards! What's wrong with you men anyway?!"

Büttner refrained from making it clear to her that he found Jesko's behaviour at least as disgusting as she did.

"Out!" insisted Julia with an outstretched finger.

"Do we believe her?" asked Hasenkrug as they went down the stairs of the hallway immediately afterwards.

"She seemed honestly shocked," Büttner replied. "Nevertheless, we can't rule out the possibility that she is a good actress who has prepared herself for exactly this situation. If she had anything to do with Gina's death, it had to be clear to her, given her social media appearances, that she would be on our radar."

"She would have had to have planned the murder in the long term," Hasenkrug said. "Moreover, she would have had to have travelled from Brandenburg and back there again for it."

"Which could be part of their plan to provide themselves with an alibi."

"Sure. But how likely is all that? Not particularly, is it?" Hasenkrug opened the doors of his official vehicle and got in on the passenger side.

"Rather unlikely," Büttner agreed with him as he too sat in the car and took the keys. "Is there any success in the Jesko Mudder case yet?"

Hasenkrug scrolled through his smartphone. "Dozens of tips from the public, but nothing conclusive so far. But now we have the forensics report from Mudder's flat. There are heaps of fingerprints from endless people, it says here. So Mudder seems to have had a lot of visitors. As already mentioned, all electronic devices – at least those that can be used for the internet – have disappeared. One or two items of women's clothing were found – blouses, panties, bras – they are all being checked for DNA."

"Any photos, documents, films that might be of interest to us?"

"There were no photos, no films either. But today they are more likely to be in digital form anyway."

Büttner started the engine and threaded his way into the traffic. "Are there no photos of women either, for example the ones that appear in the videos?" he asked. "Or at least the one of his current girlfriend Gina Gloger?"

"No. Neither on the walls nor on any dressers or in drawers. But it's not impossible that he removed them from his flat too. And if he has, it's certainly not because the women are so important to him that he absolutely has to carry their photos around with him."

Büttner sighed. "Isn't there anything interesting at all for which all the effort was worthwhile? What about his own clothes? Are they still in the flat?"

"Yes, but we don't know how many clothes he owned, although his wardrobe looks well filled when I look at the photos."

"Okay, so it's a dead end for now. Let's hope Mudder turns up soon and we can put him through the wringer."

"At least we should know soon whether he is the father of Gina's unborn child," Hasenkrug said. "That's something."

It didn't sound very hopeful, and Büttner couldn't claim to be happy with the state of the investigation so far either. But perhaps new clues would emerge at the horse farm they were now on their way to.

8

The road to the equestrian farm led David Büttner and Sebastian Hasenkrug out of Emden into the Krummhörn. Shortly after Pilsum, their sat nav sent them onto a dead-straight dirt road, and after about two kilometres, their destination was only a few hundred metres ahead of them. As far as the eye could see, the Gulfhof was surrounded by fields, meadows and paddocks that did not look particularly inviting at this time of year.

Halfway along the route, two cyclists came towards them, struggling against the fresh north-westerly wind and the never-ending November rain. Only when they were just a few metres away from them did Büttner register that they were two girls, perhaps ten years old. They looked less than enthusiastic as they swerved into the concrete driveway of a pasture and waited there until Büttner had steered his car past them. He could understand their displeasure all too well, for it was certainly no pleasure to drive across the open field in this weather, which offered them no protection whatsoever from wind and weather in this flat landscape for miles on end. Unfortunately, however, it was not possible for him to at least save them from swerving, because if he had driven on the unpaved shoulder, it would certainly have taken a tractor to pull his car out of the mud again. So he thanked them with a gesture and gave them an apologetic smile, which the children, however, did not return. A glance in the rearview mirror told him that they had got back onto their bikes and bravely continued on their way.

"Amazing," Hasenkrug remarked. "Apparently there are still parents who don't drive their children everywhere. And not even when it's storming and raining cats and dogs. That gives me back my faith in humanity."

"Do you also let your children drive through wind and weather?" Büttner inquired. "Or are you one of those who only admire other parents for it, but believe that your own child is so delicate that it could possibly melt in the rain?

"At least I'm not one of those people who call other parents' ravenous parents when they expect their children to do something," Hasenkrug countered. "Mara and Silas are not yet at the age to ride their bikes around on their own. But when they are old enough, they will be well trained, because Tonja and I have been cycling with them for a long time. It's amazing how well even our three-year-old does on them."

They drove into the cobbled courtyard entrance and immediately two completely soaked riders crossed their path, leading their horses by the halter to a barn. Apart from the main building, which traditionally consisted of the residential wing and the stable immediately adjoining it, there were two other buildings. Only one of them, which the two riders were now heading for, showed at first glance that it housed a number of horse stalls. The function of the second building, on the other hand, was not immediately clear, as its grey roller shutter was closed. It was probably a machine shed, because there were two horse trailers parked in front of it.

A woman of perhaps forty stepped out of the stable door of the farm, which was set into the high, overhanging barn door painted in the region's usual green, and eyed her curiously. She didn't seem to mind the rain that beat incessantly on her helmet-covered head. Over black, mud-spattered riding boots and brown breeches, she wore a black, fitted quilted jacket, holding a riding crop in her hand.

When Büttner and Hasenkrug got out of the car, she came towards them smiling broadly.

"Moin. You don't look like you want to take riding lessons."

"Only he wants to." Hasenkrug pointed at Büttner with a broad grin.

But he merely grimaced and then produced his badge. "Hello, Mrs … uh…"

"Grensemann. Kira Grensemann. I own this farm."

Büttner nodded and introduced himself and Hasenkrug. "We are from the criminal investigation department. It's about Gina Gloger. As we have been told, she was your riding student?"

A shadow settled on her face. "Gina, yes. I heard about her being found dead and that she was probably murdered. Word travels fast, that sort of thing. Terrible. She was such a cheerful person." Kira Grensemann pointed to a rider who was now riding into the square. "And she loved horses more than anything."

"We heard she had her own horse standing here."

"Yes. Nordwind." There was sadness in her gaze. "He senses something is wrong and he calls out to her. We try to keep him busy as much as possible to distract him. Thank goodness Sanna has been coming over more and more often to look after him for some time now. She has already taken care of Nordwind a lot in the last few years, so at least he is not completely without a caregiver now."

Büttner could not help feeling that the woman cared more about the fate of the horse than that of the murder victim. With the next gust of wind, he felt the rain make its way through the collar of his jacket and run cold down the back of his neck. "Would you mind if we continued our conversation inside?"

"No, of course not. Come in!" She pushed open the door and immediately they were standing in a huge stable, probably largely gutted at some point, which had three riding arenas strewn with sand. On all three there were a few riders, most of them on horseback, a few standing at the fences and watching.

Kira Grensemann pointed to a handsome dark-brown stallion, almost black in the legs, who was leisurely making his rounds, ridden by a red-haired woman. "That's Nordwind. An Andalusian. He has a fantastic heritage and we take him for breeding. The Gloger family has owned him for four years. As I said, he and Gina had a very intimate relationship. Only unfortunately …" She shook her head but did not speak further.

"Unfortunately?", Büttner inquired.

"Oh, I don't know either." She sighed.

Büttner noticed that she was hitting her riding crop incessantly against her lower leg with gentle strokes. What was it that made her nervous? "What don't you know?" He did not let up when she fell silent even now.

"In the last few months, Gina hasn't been here as much as before," she said hesitantly. "Sanna is sure it had something to do with her new boyfriend. She felt Gina had changed, and not for the better." The beating of her crop became more violent. "But … well, I haven't seen Jesko and Gina together much, so I can't say anything about it."

"So you know Jesko?"

"Yes. But recently … Well, no, actually, I can't say I know him particularly well."

"But the observation that Gina was not here as often as before is fact?" asked Hasenkrug, who was taking notes.

"Yes, everyone here will be able to confirm that. Whereas Gina used to be here almost every day, it's only been twice a week for the last three or four months." She strolled closer to the riding arena where Sanna and Nordwind were.

"Has she been taking riding lessons?"

"Yes, although she was already very good. I would call her a natural. Gina just succeeded at everything when it came to riding, not having to put in a lot of effort."

"She has been attending her riding lessons for the last four months, even though she hasn't been here as much?"

"Mostly, yes. Not all. Every now and then she has cancelled, which hardly ever used to happen."

Büttner was about to ask another question when his gaze fell on a rider he knew well, who was approaching them on a white horse, led by a woman he did not know. But when he opened his mouth to express his astonishment, she looked at him imploringly, raised her finger to her lips and shook her head.

What on earth was that all about? Was she possibly trying to surprise Hasenkrug, who kept his eyes on Sanna and Nordwind and then scribbled something in his notepad? Kira Grensemann turned her back on the young rider and instructed a girl of perhaps twelve to stop lunging so that she, too, would not hear anything of the silent exchange.

"Uh… now I just … what did I want to ask?" stammered Büttner, while the rider made signs to him that she would wait for him in the neighbouring building.

"Everything okay, boss?" Hasenkrug looked at him scrutinisingly.

"Yeah yeah." Büttner tried to collect himself. "Had Gina made friends here?" He remembered the question he had wanted to ask.

"Of course. Riding is a very bonding sport." Kira Grensemann laughed happily. A little too cheerfully, Büttner thought, given the current state of affairs. "For one thing, there's Sanna, of course. The two of them have always done a lot together, even outside the riding stable. And then there are Lisa and Tomke." She looked around. "I saw them earlier. I think they are in the stables taking care of the horses. Just like Gina and Sanna, they are total horse freaks, spend every spare minute here. Especially since …" She shook her head. "Well, it doesn't matter."

"Keep talking," Büttner urged her. "Every detail can be important."

She made a dismissive gesture with her hand. "No. What

I was going to say has nothing to do with Gina. It's private. It wouldn't be fair to just blurt it out here."

Büttner searched her face for signs that she was trying to hide something, but could not find anything. Maybe she really just wanted to protect the privacy of her riding students.

"How long is Sanna's riding lesson?" he asked. "We would like to talk to her."

Kira Grensemann glanced at her wristwatch. "She should be ready in about half an hour. But I could let her know that you …"

"No, no, not necessary," Büttner hurried to say, which earned him a puzzled look from his assistant. "We'll … er… have a look around here first, if you don't mind. The two friends … you said they were in the stables?"

"Yes, I suppose so, at least."

"One more question," Hasenkrug spoke up. "Do you know Eiko Harms?"

"Yes, sure. He was often here with Gina, helping her take care of Nordwind, cheering her on at tournaments … He's a sweetheart. I regretted it very much when Gina ended the relationship and joined this …" She furrowed her brow as if she couldn't think of the name.

"Jesko."

"I never understood why she turned to him of all people. His reputation precedes him, and definitely not a good one. And I can't say I'd be particularly eager to have one of my daughters with someone like him … well, thank God they're still too young to worry about men."

"How old are your daughters?" inquired Hasenkrug.

"Nine and a half and eleven. They must have actually met you on the way here."

Büttner raised his brows. "The two girls on the bikes?"

"Yes, exactly. They are on their way to Greetsiel. Went to meet up with girlfriends."

"They should be soaking wet by the time they get there."

Kira Grensemann shrugged her shoulders. "They chose it that way, they really wanted to see their friends. And I have to work. It's not too far to Greetsiel, and it's not the first time they've done it." She laughed out. "Believe me, I'm glad that I don't have such effeminate couch potatoes who only hang out in front of their tablets and lose all relationship to nature. There are already far too many of them. My girls are strong nature children, real East Frisians, and that's a good thing." She winked at Büttner. "But I'll tell you something so that you don't call the Youth Welfare Office on me after all: I'll pick them up again tonight, along with their bikes. Then they won't have to go back in the dark."

"I don't see what the Youth Welfare Office should have to do with children riding bicycles," growled Büttner.

Kira Grensemann sighed. "You wouldn't believe what parents keep the authorities busy with these days. Every single stone they try to get out of the way of their brood, even the smallest pebble. They seem to have no idea what they are doing to their children. I really wonder what will become of them." After another glance at the clock, she clapped her hands once, cautiously. "Well, now I must be off, the next riding lesson is calling." She gestured with her head towards the stable gate. "You can find your way?"

"There aren't too many opportunities to get lost here." Büttner raised his hand in greeting. "Thank you for taking the time."

"Don't mention it."

"She was quite relaxed about Gina," Hasenkrug noted when they were out of earshot.

"So you noticed that too."

"It really didn't take much. Either she doesn't care about Gina's fate, or she's one of those cheerful people who are still able to focus on the positive even in the shittiest situation."

"Which brings us to the topic," Büttner replied.

"Huh? How now? What subject?"

Büttner turned up the collar of his jacket, opened the door and stepped out into the rain, which immediately slapped him icily in the face. "Follow me, Hasenkrug. I have a surprise for you that will please you."

9

Seen from the inside, the outbuilding was larger than it appeared from the outside. David Büttner counted twelve horse stalls, separated by a concrete walkway, facing each other in two rows. In two adjacent stalls, a young woman was busy grooming a horse.

Hasenkrug looked around searchingly. "And what is the surprise now?"

Büttner had also let his gaze wander through the stable, but could not work out what he was looking for. Had he misinterpreted the rider's gesture? "Later, Hasenkrug, later." He pointed to one of the horse stalls and they walked towards it.

"I assume you are Lisa and Tomke?" asked Hasenkrug.

While the young woman in the neighbouring stall did not even turn towards them, but continued to brush her horse's coat in brisk strokes, the other woman looked at him suspiciously. When her gaze lingered on Büttner, she bristled and, exhaling heavily, closed her eyes briefly, then said, "Aren't you Jette's father by any chance?"

"You know my daughter?" Büttner could not remember having seen this young woman with the short blonde haircut before. Which meant nothing, of course, because Jette's circle of friends was largely unknown to him by now.

"Yes. She's my big sister Wilma's friend."

The name didn't mean anything to him either. "And you are?"

"Tomke. You … uh … are here about Gina, aren't you?"

"Yes. As Mrs Grensemann told us, you were friends with her."

"Then you're probably Lisa," Hasenkrug called over to the other woman, who so far still had made no move to even turn around to look at them. But she did not react to his direct address either.

Tomke grabbed her ears. "Lisa has headphones in. Listening to music."

Hasenkrug walked up to the box and tapped the woman on the shoulder. "Lisa?"

Startled, Lisa, who wore her brunette hair braided into a French plait, wheeled around, whereupon the horse also jerked its head up and began to snort nervously.

"Sorry," Hasenkrug said after Lisa had taken her wireless headphones out of her ears, "I didn't mean to scare you."

"But you did." When she also spotted Büttner, she gave her friend a questioning look.

"They are from the police," Tomke explained.

"Oh." A nervous flicker entered Lisa's eyes. "It … must be because of Gina, mustn't it?" No sooner had she spoken those words than she abruptly burst into tears. "Sorry, but it's … it's …"

"Terrible," Tomke finished her friend's sentence. "Lisa's been crying all the time. It has taken a lot out of her."

"And not you?" asked Hasenkrug.

"Yes, of course. But I … well, I …" She pressed her lips together before adding, "I'm not much for crying."

Büttner's impression was that she had actually wanted to say more. He waited to see if she would add anything else, but she remained silent.

"How did you know Gina?" he asked.

"From here. We learned to ride together. We were twelve when we started."

"Are the horses yours?"

"I wish it were so." Tomke shook her head sadly as she stroked the nostrils of the bay mare, who was feasting on oats. "But unlike Gina's parents, ours can't afford a horse." She grimaced, then specified, "Well, my father could, but he doesn't want to. We have a riding share. That's something."

"We've heard that Gina hasn't been here as often as usual in the last few months," Hasenkrug said. "Do you know why?" He handed Lisa, who wouldn't stop crying, a paper handkerchief as she rummaged searchingly in her pockets.

"Yes, that's true. She came less and less often, hardly bothered about Nordwind as a result. It was all down to Sanna." There was an unmistakable reproach in Tomke's voice. "She hardly knew us anymore either. We used to do a lot together, not only here on the farm. But in the last few months …" She shrugged her shoulders.

"What was the reason?"

Tomke laughed bitterly. "*Who* was the reason for that is probably more accurate."

Unexpectedly, Lisa burst into inane sobs. She pushed open the door of the box and ran out across the corridor into the rain.

"Gina's death really seems to have taken a toll on Lisa," Büttner noted.

"She's a sensitive one. But yeah, that really blew Lisa's mind when she …" Tomke faltered. "Well, when she heard about it."

"And who do you think was the reason that Gina had withdrawn?", Hasenkrug repeated his question.

"Jesko, of course. Jesko Mudder. I'm sure you've heard of him, right?"

"So you're assuming it was Jesko who kept Gina out of here?"

Tomke twisted the corners of her mouth mockingly. "If you want to put it that way. But in the end, Gina decided for herself what she wanted and what she didn't want. And all this," she made an expansive movement with her arms, "she apparently didn't want any more."

"Do you know Jesko Mudder personally?" asked Hasenkrug.

"Yes, unfortunately." Tomke rolled her eyes. "He's one of those the world doesn't need. No matter where or with whom he shows up, he leaves behind a stinking pile of crap."

"From what we have heard, women still like him."

"Nope, nope, nope!" she cried in a flurry. "*Not all* women don't like him! But that's typical again, generalizing, just because the guy's always hooking up with someone else."

"Isn't it the case that at least these women also willingly *let* themselves be picked up by him?", Büttner formulated his retort in a deliberately provocative way.

"Yeah, sure. And the very ones who are too stupid to realise what a full-on jerk Jesko is." She slapped her forehead with the flat of her hand. "Honestly, how stupid do you have to be to still fall for that one!"

"Did you ever see him and Gina together?"

"Once. At a party. And honestly? It was disgusting! The way Gina threw herself at him … just disgusting! If you ask me, she was completely smitten with him. Really want to know what he had, that a woman as intelligent as Gina, would fall for him." Her voice softened as she added after a short pause, "She wasn't like that. Actually, she was quite different. I don't know what happened to her. Really, I don't." To Büttner's amazement, her eyes filled with tears. "I … I'm so sorry." She slapped her hands in front of her face, sobbing.

"Sorry for what?"

It took a while before Tomke regained her composure. "Well, that Gina is dead, what else?" she sniffled, and now she too was handed a handkerchief by Hasenkrug.

"Do you have any idea who might be responsible for her death?" asked Büttner after she had blown her nose.

"Jesko. Who else," it came without hesitation.

Büttner's mobile beeped. Looking at the display, he couldn't help smiling. "Okay," he said, "we have to go. Thank you for taking the time to talk to us." He slipped her a business card. "If you think of anything else, please get back to me." He looked around searchingly. "Is there another stable here with stalls?"

"Nah, not one like this one." Tomke pointed to a door behind the row of stalls, which Büttner only now noticed. "But behind it is the free run for the horses, with a connection to the outdoor area. So they can decide for themselves whether they want to be inside or outside." A barely perceptible smile played around the corners of her mouth. "Today they prefer to stay inside." She patted her mare's flank. "Even my whirlwind Sunny, who usually can't be outside enough, doesn't fancy this sour weather. Right, Sunny?"

The horse snorted as if it understood her.

"I find it difficult to assess Tomke's emotional state," Hasenkrug remarked as they stepped through the door into the free stall. "A mixture of anger and sadness, I would say. Whereas the anger still seems to predominate. But what exactly is she angry at? At Jesko for alienating their friend? At Gina, because she felt abandoned by her? Or is it …" Hasenkrug fell silent. Probably because his jaw dropped when he saw the rider, who now, led by another woman, came riding towards them on her white horse and called out to them with a grin: "Moin. Do you want to join me?"

"Marieke?" breathed Hasenkrug barely audibly.

"Shh!" Büttner told him to shut up. Then he murmured to him, "Yes, that's how I looked when I saw her earlier. But apparently she doesn't want us to know her. If you know what I mean."

"So this is the surprise you were talking about. Well, boss, I must say you have succeeded."

"Hello," Büttner greeted after clearing his throat. He pulled out his service card. "My name is Büttner, this is my colleague Hasenkrug. We are from the criminal investigation department. Mrs Grensemann told us we could find you here."

Marieke acted surprised. "Criminal investigation department? What's it about?"

"I'm sure it's about Gina," said her riding instructor – or whatever function the woman had here.

"But I didn't even know Gina."

"Anyway. That's enough for today. After all, we don't want to overexert you. Come on, I'll help you dismount." The woman nodded at Büttner. "You'll excuse us for a moment? Marieke will be right back with you."

The two disappeared into an adjoining room together with the horse. Several minutes later, Marieke, now sitting in a wheelchair, came out the door alone again. "Whew!" She wiped the sweat from her forehead as she finally brought the wheelchair to a halt in front of them. "Riding is quite exhausting."

"I didn't know that was possible if you can't walk," Büttner wondered. He looked around the stable, but they seemed to be alone, except for about a dozen horses. So they could speak freely.

"Oh, walking gets better every day, boss. Mostly my crutches are enough for me now." Marieke laughed, but her exhaustion was evident. "Jelka has kept me quite busy these last two months. Thank goodness for that. Without her, I'd probably still be sitting in a wheelchair, dully mourning my fate."

"I don't know that you ever did," Hasenkrug put it into perspective. "But congratulations, Marieke, soon you'll be running away from us all again!"

Büttner was pleased that bringing Jelka, who would soon be competing in her first Paralympics, and Marieke together seemed to bring about exactly what Hasenkrug and he had hoped for. If this rapid progress continued, Marieke would be back at work in the foreseeable future. Which would be a blessing, as she was sorely missed by everyone. And her serious accident could then finally be forgotten.

After Büttner had made sure once more that no one was eavesdropping on them, he said, "But let's get something straight, Marieke: Surely it's no coincidence that you're here."

"Of course not." Marieke grinned. "I read about our new case in the press and concluded that a bit of riding therapy definitely couldn't hurt me."

"Uh…" Büttner was once again amazed at how quickly his young colleague managed to make connections. "But how did you know that this riding stable … I mean, there was nothing about it in the press, as far as I know."

"Nah, but on the internet." She grinned cheekily at Büttner. "It's something like the daily paper, only in modern, you know? If you want, I'll show it to you sometime."

Büttner refrained from making a pointed remark.

"If you go through Gina's social media channels, you will quickly find out where she has been and with whom. So it's no big deal to come across this riding stable as well. That is why I thought I'd take a look around here." Marieke winked at Büttner. "And I was very curious to see how long it would take you to come up with the same idea."

"So are we living up to your expectations?"

Marieke stuck both thumbs in the air. "I'm very impressed, boss. I didn't expect to see you until tomorrow at the earliest."

"Your commitment is honourable, Marieke," said Hasenkrug, "but … how did you do it again? I mean, you don't get riding therapy overnight, do you?"

"That's right. But if you just want to see if it's something for you – trial lesson, you understand – then all you need is to reach for the phone, a bit of tear-jerking, a bit of infatuation with horses and – whoops! – you're sitting on the back of one. And I didn't even have to fib about the latter because I've always liked horses. Like almost all girls. I started taking riding lessons when I was twelve. I stayed with them for about two years, then I got fed up with the constant fuss about tournaments and stuff."

"And what is the higher purpose for your presence here?" Büttner inquired.

"It's obvious, boss. I'll ask around a bit, pick up opinions, see who stood by Gina. Undercover, of course, otherwise I won't find out anything."

"And how is that supposed to work? You've had your trial lesson now and …"

"You let me worry about that, boss," Marieke didn't let him finish.

"Hm." Büttner knew it would serve no purpose to draw Marieke's attention to her sick leave. If he was honest with himself, he didn't want to, because they could use her help. Although he did not know at this point whether the riding stable was at all relevant to their case, with Marieke on board they would surely find out soon enough. He knew no one who could gather information faster than she could, not to mention the razor-sharp conclusions she drew from it.

"So, and now you'd best talk to my riding therapist," Marieke said. "Her name is Silvia. Not that anyone wonders why you're questioning me when I've only been here since today and don't care about veteran staff."

"Ay, ay, Käpt'n," Hasenkrug grinned.

Büttner raised his hand. "First of all, we will now talk to this Sina …"

"Sanna," Hasenkrug corrected him.

"Anyway, we will talk to her now. Her riding lesson should be over."

"I understand that you have already spoken to Lisa and Tomke," Marieke said.

"With Tomke, yes," Hasenkrug confirmed. "Not with Lisa, she couldn't speak because of her grief.

"Did Tomke contribute anything enlightening?"

"She thinks Jesko Mudder, Gina's boyfriend, killed her. Like everyone we've spoken to so far actually. At least everyone seems to think the worst of this man." Hasenkrug brought Marieke up to speed on the investigation in a few short sentences.

"Jesko Mudder it is, okay." Marieke made a note on her smartphone. "I'll try to find out something about him." She yawned. "So, guys, I'm going to have my mother pick me up now. I'm really through."

Büttner noticed Kira Grensemann enter the hall and approach her. "Good, Ms de Boer," he said to Marieke, "then we wish you a continued good recovery."

"Thank you, Commissioner. I'm sorry I couldn't be of more help to you. But, as I said, I've only been here since today and I didn't know Gina at all."

"No problem. We just want to make sure we don't miss anything."

"I didn't want to disturb you, but I see you're just saying goodbye," Kira Grensemann interjected into the conversation. "Sanna's riding lesson is over now. I told her that you still wanted to talk to her. She is waiting for you in the riding hall."

"Thank you, that's nice. Yes, well, thank you again, Ms de Boer, and no hard feelings."

"No problem. You're welcome."

"So, Marieke, now we can discuss how to proceed with your therapy," Büttner heard the stud manager say as they made their way to the exit.

"What a coup by Marieke," Hasenkrug said admiringly as they walked through the rain back to the Gulfhof. "Again." He brushed the drops out of his hair. "Whew, I'm glad her health keeps going up. Who would have thought."

Büttner nodded in agreement. This had not been expected. When he thought of Marieke's resuscitation alone, which he had had to witness in hospital only a few months ago – phew! His knees still became weak when the horrible images came back to his mind.

Talk about weak knees! Before Büttner entered the riding hall, he checked his smartphone. Jette should have been in the air by now. Last night she had downloaded an app for him to follow her flight. He breathed a sigh of relief when the dot he was looking for appeared on the display. The plane with Jette on board was somewhere over the Alps at that time.

"Have a good flight, little one," he murmured. "And arrive safely in Cape Town."

10

Sanna was standing outside the riding arena with a young man when David Büttner and Sebastian Hasenkrug returned to the riding hall. The two seemed familiar with each other because he had his arm around her shoulder and was whispering something in her ear. He was also wearing riding clothes and cut a good figure in them. Büttner assumed that with his fashionably cut blond hair, angular face with three-day beard and athletic figure, he certainly went down well with the women. But there was no sign of Gina's stallion Nordwind, whom Sanna had ridden before. Apparently someone had already led him out.

When the young man saw the two commissioners coming towards him, he pushed Sanna away from him as if he was embarrassed to be seen with her. Nor did he make any move to leave, but took two steps towards them and held out his hand.

"Moin," he said with a smile that was as put on as it was condescending when Büttner shook his hand. "You're from the criminal investigation department, aren't you? My mother already said that you still wanted to talk to Sanna."

"Your mother?"

"Yes. Kira Grensemann."

"Ah." Büttner estimated the man to be in his early twenties, which was a significant age difference from his two sisters. So Kira Grensemann should also be older than the forty he had estimated her to be. Or had she just been a young mother? "And your name is?"

"Christopher Grensemann." Looking proud, he seemed to be hoping for some kind of reaction. In fact, the name meant nothing to Büttner, nor did he know any reason why he should have recognised him.

"Ah!" Hasenkrug tapped his forehead. "You are the show jumper who is currently making a splash at the national level, right?"

This choice of words seemed to please Grensemann, as he pumped out his chest. "I have just won the national title in several disciplines. Next up is the European Championships. I'm certainly not exaggerating when I say that my chances are good to win a title there as well."

"Congratulations. I saw it on television. An impressive achievement."

Büttner wondered why Hasenkrug was even buttering up this obviously self-absorbed guy. Didn't he notice that he was only eager to brag about his successes? "Did you know Gina Gloger?" he asked, to end the creepy self-promotion once and for all. After all, they were not in the sports TV studio.

"Of course." Grensemann tried hard to look sad, but he didn't quite want to succeed. "Gina was a great person and an even greater rider. It's a shame that she can no longer compete for our stable."

"I see." Success in equestrian sport seemed to be all that

interested this man. "And from the human aspect? What was your relationship with Gina?"

Grensemann frowned and put his hand to his chin in thinker's pose, which was probably meant to give him an intellectual air. "I think that Gina and I had a very special relationship. We were," he swayed his head back and forth, "yes, I would say we were soul mates." He looked at Sanna, who stood beside him looking embarrassed. "Don't you think so, Sanna? Between Gina and me, there … yes, there were those special vibes." He put his arm around her and pulled her close. "Which is not to say that my fiery witch Sanna and I aren't a happy couple." As if to confirm his words, he pressed a kiss to her cheek.

The 'fiery witch' brushed one of her red curls behind her ear and nodded silently, looking anything but happy.

"I'm less interested in the special vibes or any kind of soul mates," Büttner replied. "You may have lost a spiritually inclined poet, Mr Grensemann, but unfortunately I have to bring you down to earth now. Gina Gloger was murdered. Her body is lying on the forensic medicine table. It doesn't get much less romantic than that. Despite your alleged affinity with her, however, you don't give the impression that this fact is particularly close to your heart."

"Yes, of course it does go to my heart, as it does to all of ours. But life goes on, doesn't it? Gina certainly wouldn't have wanted us to stand here and mope. She would have wanted us to ride, have fun and win trophies." Grensemann nodded as if he had to confirm these unctuous words to himself. He seemed to enjoy his role – however he defined it for himself.

"Where were you the night Gina was murdered? Say between twenty and twenty-two pm on Monday."

Grensemann looked at him irritated. "You don't seriously want an alibi from me now." He phrased it as a statement, not a question.

"Yes, that's exactly what I want. So?"

"By Sanna." Again, he encircled her with his arm. "Isn't that right, my darling?" He winked conspiratorially at Büttner and Hasenkrug. "If you know what I mean."

Heavens, this guy was disgusting! Büttner wondered how a woman as patient as Kira Grensemann could have given birth to such a snob. What had gone wrong?

"Can you confirm that?" asked Hasenkrug, addressing Sanna.

She nodded but said nothing.

"You have your own flat?"

"No. I still live with my parents. But they're on holiday." She blushed to the roots, which made an interesting combination with her red hair.

"And you?", Büttner turned to her friend. "Do you also still live with mum and dad?"

Grensemann did not seem to like this formulation, for he grimaced sourly. "This farm is big enough for all of us," he replied, which was probably a yes.

"Well, now that that's settled, we'd like to talk to Sanna … uh … what was your last name again?"

"Visser," replied Christopher Grensemann.

"I assume that your friend would have known her surname herself. So, Mr Grensemann, if you would please leave us alone then."

"It is also Sanna's wish that I stay, and …", Grensemann continued to contradict.

"I don't know if you've noticed," Büttner drove into his parade in an unusually sharp tone, "but your girlfriend is an adult, and your type is no longer wanted here."

"I beg your pardon!"

"Go complain to your mother but go!"

Grensemann gave his girlfriend a prompting look. Apparently he expected her to confirm his supposed wish, but she only lowered her eyes and maltreated her lower lip with her teeth. "Very well, Sanna, I'll see you later," he said. Had there been a threat? Finally he stalked off and disappeared out the door.

"I would like a drink of water," Sanna said in a thin voice. She gestured to two benches that stood near the door. "My bottle is in my backpack. Is that all right?"

"Of course, no problem." Büttner would also have liked something to drink now, preferably a warming coffee, because he was shivering here in the riding stable. But that would have to wait.

Sanna wiped the sweat from her forehead with a towel she had dug out of her backpack, then put her aluminium bottle to her mouth and drank. Riding seemed to have exerted her.

"Do you also ride in tournaments?" asked Büttner, trying to find a way into the conversation.

"Yes, of course, we all ride tournaments. That's part of it, isn't it?" It didn't exactly sound like overflowing enthusiasm.

"We are told that you were close friends with Gina Gloger. Is that right?"

"I thought so too, yes." Sanna, who suddenly appeared much more confident than in the presence of her boyfriend, pointed to the benches. "Please, won't you sit down?"

"Thank you." Büttner and Hasenkrug took their seats. "What did you want to imply with your remark?"

"That we were friends at some point. Yes, I think I was even Gina's best friend. But then … well." Her eyes darkened. "It was all good. Until Jesko came along. Suddenly she had no time for me. And no time for anyone else either. Not even for Nordwind. Which was pretty shitty of her." Sighing, she sank down on the bench next to her.

Jesko Mudder again. So far, all witnesses seemed to agree that he had exerted an unhealthy influence on Gina.

"Mrs Grensemann told us that you have also always cared a lot about Nordwind," Hasenkrug said.

"Yes." Her eyes began to shine. "He's a great horse. Not just at shows – where he's really brilliant – but in general. He has a great character, is very affectionate and sensitive. For me, there is nothing better than riding out with him. We are a really good team."

"Then you should be quite happy to be able to ride him even more often from now on," Hasenkrug said. Even if it was a little arrogant to make such a statement, Büttner knew what his assistant was getting at.

Sanna saw through his tactics and scowled at him. "You don't think I killed Gina because of Nordwind and some trophies, do you?"

"Did you?" asked Büttner.

"Nonsense." The gleam departed from her eyes as quickly as it had come. She snorted indignantly. "What good was that going to do either? Or do you perhaps think that Nordwind is now just mine?"

"You don't want to take it over?"

Sanna looked at him contemptuously. "It's really not about wanting. How much do you think a great horse like that costs?!" Her look turned sad. "I for one could never afford him."

"Maybe your parents?"

"No, them even less. Not everyone has as much money as the Glogers." Envy was unmistakable between the lines, but also a certain amount of contempt.

"Does that mean that Nordwind is now being sold?" inquired Hasenkrug. "Doesn't anyone else from Gina's family ride?"

"Nah, none of them." Sanna swallowed hard. "Yes, I think they will sell Nordwind. But maybe … well … maybe someone here at the stud will find someone to buy him. Then he could stay. That would be great, of course." She let her now tear-veiled gaze wander searchingly through the riding hall, as if this someone had to come around the corner at any moment.

"I heard from Christopher's words that Gina not only had a great horse, but was also a fantastic rider," Hasenkrug said. "Did she win many competitions?"

Sanna nodded. "All the time. Gina was the figurehead of this riding stable, so to speak."

"I thought that was Christopher," Büttner growled.

"With the men, yes. With the women, clearly Gina was the most successful." Either she deliberately missed his sarcastic tone, or she was not receptive to it.

"Is that why you're with Christopher?"

"What?"

"Because he's successful. And wealthy."

She paused for a moment, then said snottily, "I really don't see how that's any of your business."

Büttner had to admit that he had initially misjudged Sanna. If he had assumed that she was a shy, easily manipulated young woman, he was now inclined to revise this view. But was she really so calculating that she got involved with such a self-centred guy because he not only had money but also great influence in the equestrian scene? Was she hoping that this liaison would boost her own sporting career? Was she perhaps no less selfish than Grensemann?

"Is there anyone you would believe to have murdered Gina?" asked Hasenkrug.

"Jesko, who else," she answered promptly.

"What motive do you think he should have had?"

"He doesn't need a motive to go completely berserk."

Well, that statement was not particularly helpful. "Can you be a little more specific?"

"Well, Jesko is a total choleric when things don't go his way."

"But you can't tell us whether there was or could have been a specific occasion. Anything you observed or overheard between the two of them or anything like that."

"Nah, I don't know." She shrugged lamely. "After all, I wasn't there when he …" She swallowed hard, and her body shuddered. "When Gina … was murdered." The last two words came out of her in a whisper.

"And you maintain that you were with Christopher at that time?", Hasenkrug inquired.

She glared at him angrily. "Why would he lie?"

Büttner sighed. "Believe me, from experience, that's what people do most often in murder investigations. For whatever motive."

"It was like Christopher told you," Sanna insisted. "We were together at the time and definitely not … with Gina." It sounded defiant.

"Were there people here in the riding stable with whom Gina didn't get along so well?" asked Büttner. "Anyone who envied her success, for example?"

"Not that I know of." Sanna frowned. "Although … the other day, last weekend at Kira's birthday party, she had a fight. With Holger. A pretty big fight, actually. I was really afraid he'd do something to Gina. He was really pissed off."

"Who is Holger?", Hasenkrug wanted to know.

"Holger Moersler. He works here as a jack-of-all-trades. Stable boy, caretaker, gardener, driver… anything that is needed."

"And what was the argument about?"

"I don't know exactly. Holger had a huge crush on Gina. For a long time now. But she kept turning him down. He was drunk that night. I don't know what she did to drive him up the wall."

"So Gina turned up to the party even though she wasn't usually here that much?"

"Yes. She was there with Jesko. He always shows up wherever there's free food and drink."

"Then jealousy could have been the reason for the altercation, couldn't it?"

"Yes, it can be."

"How did things turn out?"

Sanna pursed her mouth. "One-nil for Holger. He rammed his fist into Jesko's face at some point, Jesko was knocked out, that was it."

"He was knocked out?"

Sanna nodded.

"That means there was an emergency medical call?"

"No. It wasn't that bad. Someone threw a bucket of cold water over Jesko's face and he was back up again."

"Do you know where this Holger is now?"

"Left him with Nordwind to rub down and groom. He will be in the box with him. I usually do that myself, but now you insisted on talking to me." The hidden reproach was unmistakable.

Büttner couldn't help feeling that no one at this equestrian farm really seemed to care that Gina was dead. Except maybe Lisa, who seemed to be honestly grieving.

"All right, Ms … er…" Büttner rose. Slowly he was getting too cold to stay in the riding hall, his initial chill had long since turned into a full-blown freeze. "That's it for now." He handed her a business card as well. "Just in case."

They walked over to the horse stalls again, but there was no one to be seen for miles, just like next door. Nordwind was standing in the free stall, just like the horses Tomke and Lisa had taken care of and was eating a portion of oats.

"Are you looking for anyone in particular?" Kira Grensemann had stepped behind her. She was still holding her riding crop in her hand, still hitting it gently against her leg. Was this possibly some kind of tick?

"Holger Moersler," Hasenkrug replied.

She didn't seem to like this answer for some reason because her expression darkened visibly. "I'm sorry. Holger isn't here anymore. He finished early today."

"Is there a reason for that?"

"Something is going on with his sick mother. He has to take care of her. That happens from time to time. As long as he does his job well, he can make it as flexible as he wants. And he does."

"That means he's not coming back today either?"

"I assume so, yes. But tomorrow you're sure to meet him here again." She looked from one to the other. "What is it about?"

"What was his relationship to Gina?", Büttner asked a question in turn.

"What are you getting at? Holger works here and Gina is … was one of our riding students."

"So they only knew each other superficially?"

"Just the way people know each other in such circumstances."

Why was she evading a concrete answer? "So there was no disagreement between the two?"

"Not that I know of." Her gaze became lurking, as if she were trying to gauge what they knew and didn't know. When Büttner continued to eye her expectantly, she finally smacked her forehead with the flat of her hand. "Oh, surely Sanna told you about the incident at my birthday party, is that it?"

"Why don't you just tell us what happened at this party?"

Kira Grensemann looked unsettled. Was she wondering whether she had betrayed something with this statement that should have remained a secret?

"Oh, it was nothing really," she explained hesitantly. "For some reason Holger and Jesko got into a fight. There was probably too much alcohol involved and they egged each other on. That's the way it is at a party. At some point Holger's fist landed in Jesko's face and he went down." She made a throwing gesture with her hand. "But that was probably due to the alcohol level rather than the force of the punch. A bucket of water fixed it. I then called two taxis, one for Jesko and one for Holger, and that was it."

It didn't help, they would have to ask Holger Moersler about it themselves, because quite obviously Kira Grensemann was interested in playing down the incident.

"And if it was him?" asked Hasenkrug when they were on their way to the car a little later. It was raining cats and dogs, and the wind had picked up again, chasing an armada of dark clouds. Accordingly, they were in a hurry to get out of the rain.

"If who was what?" growled Büttner in a bad mood. His body was one big lump of ice. If he didn't get warm quickly, he would have a fat cold by tomorrow at the latest. He started the engine and switched the heating to the highest setting.

"If the incident was really nothing more than a banal brawl between two testosterone-charged men."

"Then that's exactly what I'd like to hear from Moersler." Büttner cursed because he could hardly see anything through the fogged-up windscreen; which could end bitterly in view of the only moderately wide dirt road. So he also turned up the ventilation. "My gut tells me otherwise, though." He growled indignantly. "Most importantly, it tells me I'm hungry. So I'll call it a day after I drop you off at the commissariat. We'll deal with Moersler tomorrow."

They had reached the county road and he turned left towards Emden.

11

"You are looking in such a good mood, boss," his assistant wondered when David Büttner entered the office the next morning. "Did Jette turn around halfway to Cape Town to take remorseful refuge in her father's arms?"

"No, but she arrived safely in Cape Town. Debbie, whom she describes as a delightful person, met her at the airport, and Jette wrote in her last message that she was dead tired, but everything at her temporary home, which is within walking distance of the beach, was beautiful and relaxed." Büttner sank down on his desk chair, holding a cup of coffee in his hand.

"Have you heard anything from Jette this morning?"

"No, why? She'll want to sleep it off after the long journey."

"I'm just saying. Not that Debbie turned into a werewolf overnight and ate her. After all, it was a full moon."

Büttner grimaced. "You used to be funnier, Hasenkrug." He took a sip of coffee. "What's the news from the investigation front? Do we finally have a usable lead on the whereabouts of this … er… Josef."

"Jesko Mudder?" Hasenkrug shook his head. "No. He has still disappeared off the face of the earth. However, there are new results from the forensic investigation that should make him the prime suspect. According to these, we can assume ninety-nine percent that Gina drowned in Jesko's bathtub. Among other things, small traces of blood were found on the floor of the bathroom, which undoubtedly came from Gina. Although every effort was made to cover up any traces – the bathroom was thoroughly cleaned – but as we know, even the most ambitious house cleaning doesn't stand a chance against our technical devices."

"Blood?" Büttner frowned. "So she was not only drowned, but also injured?"

"I guess we have to assume that, then, yes. I've already spoken to Anja Wilkens about it, but she says it's impossible to say what wounds Gina sustained and when because of the condition of the body."

"This means that the traces do not necessarily have to come from that evening," Büttner stated.

"Not necessarily, no. Since Gina had been in Jesko's flat almost every day for the last few months, the blood doesn't necessarily have to be connected to the murder."

"Mudder could have beaten her up before," Büttner pondered aloud. "Hadn't one of our witnesses claimed that he was a choleric person?"

Hasenkrug leafed through his notes. "Yes, Sanna Visser said that. This theory could also be supported by the fact that small traces of her blood were found not only in the bathroom but elsewhere as well."

"Maybe one of those," Büttner drew inverted commas in the air, "regrettable slips that beating partners always feel so sorry for afterwards. But that's of no use to us for our evidence for the time being. So what do forensics suggest that the murder took place in Mudder's flat?"

"A necklace was found in a small basket on the bathtub shelf. Gina's parents testified that it was a high school graduation present from her grandmother and that Gina had come home especially that day to get this necklace. She wanted to wear it for some occasion."

"Does anyone know what the occasion was?"

"We are still trying to find out. Gina probably didn't tell her parents anything specific when they asked her about it. But the fact is that Gina must have been at Jesko's flat after her brief appearance at her parents'."

Büttner sighed, "No. The fact is that the necklace was in the flat. Which suggests that Gina was there too, but it's not a foregone conclusion. And the necklace doesn't point to the murder at all."

"That is correct," Hasenkrug agreed with him. "But it is also a fact that the necklace, and especially the pendant, have traces of bath foam on them. Bath foam, of which a half-empty bottle was found in Mudder's bathroom and which – as has already been confirmed by forensic medicine – was also found in Gina's lungs. The pendant on this necklace is quite large, by the way." Hasenkrug played up the picture of the pendant on the new screen.

"A tree of life carved in wood," Büttner noted. "Pretty."

"Yes. And not only were bath foam traces found on this tree of life, but also Gina's fingerprints – which in turn cover up the bath foam traces. But other people's fingerprints are not on it."

"Hm. So Gina wore the necklace in the bathtub? That won't have done the wood any good."

"She might have forgotten to take the necklace off, realised it at some point and made up for it."

"However, this is still not proof of the murder."

"No. But circumstantial evidence in a valid chain of reasoning, I think."

Büttner shrugged his shoulders lamely. He didn't quite know what to make of this hint yet. All this was still far too vague for him. "And what about traces of other people? If we assume that there were actually two people involved in the murder, then there should be traces of them as well. Fingerprints, DNA, fibres …"

"As I said, the whole bathroom was thoroughly cleaned before the forensics were in there," Hasenkrug replied. "At least the tiles and other surfaces. The bottle with the bath foam, on which Gina's fingerprints are also found, on the other hand, was not wiped off."

"And the chain was also left lying around instead of being removed from the bathroom?" wondered Büttner.

"Probably no importance was attached to it. It was not the only thing in the basket. Rather, it was a hodgepodge of random bits and pieces." Hasenkrug also played in a picture of the basket. Rings, chains, condoms, buttons, stones …

"Very well," said Büttner. "The overall picture allows for the train of thought that it could have been as you say. Whether it would be enough for the judge to formulate a guilty verdict, I would likely doubt."

"Mark Humboldt agrees that the procedure indicates

that the clean-up was not particularly well thought out and was therefore probably carried out under stress. It was cleaned thoroughly, but the details were overlooked."

"When I have to clean our bathroom at home, it also causes me stress," said Büttner. "And with the details, I don't have it the way my wife would like it either. What I'm saying is: maybe the bathroom was just subjected to routine cleaning. There's supposed to be." Büttner was still not completely convinced by Hasenkrug's theory, though he did not want to rule out the possibility that it might have been so. "Be that as it may. If it's the way you and Mark Humboldt made it up, all we need is someone to blame for all this. Is there really no one who claims to have seen Jesko Mudder after the murder?"

"There are even a lot of people who still want to have seen him. Every clue is being followed up. But so far, every single one has turned out to be a loser."

"Well then, I guess there's not much more we can do than wait and see. What else is there?"

"I checked Julia Vogler's alibi."

Büttner scratched his forehead.

"The young lady who claims to have been on a houseboat in Brandenburg for a week," Hasenkrug jogged his memory.

The penny dropped for Büttner. "And? Was she?"

"Yes. Everything Julia has posted on social media in the meantime indicates that her story is true."

"Photos can be faked."

"Exactly. That's why I put some colleagues on it. On the one hand, the forensics department assumes that the photos have not been tampered with. On the other hand, the houseboat rental company confirms that the houseboat was rented under her name at the time stated by Julia and that it did not dock again in its home port for the entire week. In addition, nothing actually happened on all her social media accounts for a week after Julia had announced her time off there. Her mobile phone was also switched off for the entire period. Until just before we showed up at her place."

"She could have parked the houseboat somewhere else in between and used a different mobile phone," Büttner indicated.

"Houseboats don't park, they moor."

Büttner grunted indignantly. "Your quibbles don't get us one step further, Hasenkrug."

"But even you have to admit that it doesn't look so bad for Julia's alibi, chief."

"At least until it is disproved." Büttner squinted at his desk drawer. Should he treat himself to a chocolate bar?

"Don't even think about it, boss!"

Büttner felt caught. "Stop reading my mind, Hasenkrug! That's encroaching."

"Jette has arrived well in Cape Town and will have a good time there," his assistant countered. "So there is no reason to take refuge in old patterns out of concern for her."

Büttner pulled a face. "Has anyone ever told you that you're a fucking buzzkill, Hasenkrug?"

"Yes, you've said it a thousand times. But go ahead and say it again, lest I forget. Can we now … Shit, that was Mrs Weniger!"

Suddenly a scream was heard from the antechamber, then loud thumping. Büttner and Hasenkrug jumped up at the same time and rushed to the door. Before they opened it, Hasenkrug drew his gun while Büttner was still thinking about where he had deposited his. At a signal, Hasenkrug yanked the door open, leapt forward with his gun outstretched and …

"Oops!"

After a few seconds of shock had passed, Marieke, who was standing in front of them leaning on crutches, burst out laughing. "Now that's what I call commitment, boys!" She winked at Frau Weniger. "At least you don't have to worry about your safety, it seems."

Hasenkrug grimaced but couldn't help grinning either. "Marieke! What a surprise! I can't say I expected you."

"I should hope so, because otherwise the gun pointed at me would have really given me pause for thought," she countered.

"May I ask why you are shouting so loudly and scaring us to death with it, Mrs Weniger?" grumbled Büttner. He looked with a furrowed brow at a pile of broken pieces lying in a brown puddle on the ground, along with scattered soil and a tattered-looking plant.

"Oh, I was just so surprised to see Marieke here, and without her wheelchair. And because I was so happy, I jumped up wildly with my arms and knocked over the flowerpot – and then my coffee mug got knocked over, too." She told it so radiantly, as if this mishap was one of the highlights of her life.

"What brings you here, Marieke?" asked Büttner, while

Hasenkrug set about sweeping up the broken pieces. After another glance at the floor, he added: "Would you like a coffee?"

"You're welcome. Thank you."

"Go on into the office, I'll bring you the coffee." Mrs Weniger's radiance seemed to be frozen in her face. Just like all of them, the weeks of worry about Marieke had taken their toll on her. So it was all the nicer that they could now all breathe a sigh of relief together. Their young colleague was still far from being one hundred percent recovered, but she would make it the rest of the way.

12

"Wow, where did that rad thing come from all of a sudden?!" asked Marieke as soon as they had entered the office. "Surely modernity isn't suddenly going to move in here?"

"We are still working on coping with this unexpected development," Büttner replied. "The fact that there are still such things as positive surprises even in our agency is something you first have to digest." He pushed a chair towards Marieke, on which she sighed with relief and dropped her walking aids. "You can sit on our table again later," he alluded to her favourite seat with a wink.

Hasenkrug came in and handed her the steaming mug of coffee. "And," he said, "surely you're not here to stop us from working."

"Nah. More like I'm here to bring you work." She pulled out a USB stick and handed it to Hasenkrug. "Here, you can put it on the fancy new monitor."

The first thing that appeared on the screen was a photo of Jesko Mudder. "I did a little research on him and asked around my circle of friends under the pretext of a fictitious occasion if anyone knew him," Marieke explained. "All in all, the guy is not exactly known as a popular figure, to put it mildly. Nevertheless, he has many admirers, especially among women. He has never had a lack of affairs, mostly at the same time. Which in turn commands respect and also envy from many a man, as you can imagine."

Büttner nodded. "That confirms the impression we got. What about his porn site? That could be the crux of the murder. Have you found anyone who claims to have known about this website?"

"I didn't ask for it directly so as not to jeopardise our investigation."

Büttner swallowed hard as tears of relief rose in him after her words. Marieke had said 'our investigation'. She was indeed back in the game. He had hardly dared to hope.

"Is something wrong, boss, that you're looking at me so strangely?" inquired Marieke.

"No. It's all good." He gave her an encouraging nod. "So what about the porn site now?"

"Well, a sensitive subject, I would say. I didn't want to go public with it and start rumours that might hinder our investigations. Do we know anything about the site's subscribers yet?"

"We are still waiting for the evaluation of the forensics," Hasenkrug answered. "That means that at the moment we know as little about the subscribers as we do about the women Mudder abused for this. Except Julia Vogler, of course."

"Okay." Marieke nodded in confirmation. "As long as we don't know more, we'd better not startle anyone."

"I would be surprised if that hadn't happened long ago," Hasenkrug qualified. "After all, the page has been blocked by the public prosecutor's office. When you open it, a corresponding notice appears. Whoever opens this website will have realised long ago that there might be a problem.

"Yes, of course," Marieke agreed with him. "Still, this customer is hardly going to write a letter to the editor to the newspaper complaining that his favourite toy has been taken away from him. Also, I can hardly imagine that one knows about the other. The fact that a man consumes porn sites is something he doesn't usually advertise."

"If people find out that there were women on this page who they might know personally or who might even be related to them, then the dynamic that is created could be one that can no longer be controlled," Büttner feared. "It could even lead to calls for vigilante justice. Especially since the women apparently knew nothing about it."

"Which could be one reason why Jesko Mudder has gone underground," Hasenkrug concluded. "Most likely he suspects that he is in real trouble, regardless of whether he committed the murder of Gina or not."

Büttner screwed up his face. "What a disgusting story."

"Let Jesko get his ass in a sling," Marieke said pitilessly. "If he had thought with his brain instead of his dick for a change, he wouldn't have a problem now."

Hasenkrug nodded. "Just like those who consumed his site."

"Still, none of this explains why Gina had to die," Büttner returned to the murder case. "Unless she was involved in the whole enterprise."

"You mean she supported the porn site?" asked Hasenkrug. "From everything we know so far, I wouldn't think that's very likely."

Marieke also shook her head. "I've already checked that out too. The fact is that Gina and Jesko never had much to do with each other. Until Jesko started hitting on her a few months ago. Probably needed some fresh meat for his porn shit. Heaven knows why Gina fell for his scam in the end. But it is extremely unlikely that she had anything to do with the porn site. However, there is something else that should be of burning interest to you …"

"Oh, sorry, Marieke, but something just came in from forensics," Hasenkrug interrupted her. "They sent the porn site's client list. In addition, a few of the … hm … nude actresses were identified because someone here at the police station recognised them. But we now have the first names of all the other women."

"They're hardly the true ones, are they?" Marieke expressed her doubts.

"For the customers, Mudder gave the women fake names, that's right. Lola, Nikki, Vivi … the usual stuff. But in the file names, apparently the real first names show up. We don't have any surnames though."

"Can you play the lists with the names of the clients on the screen?" asked Büttner.

"Sure." The very next moment, Jesko's photo was replaced by an Excel spreadsheet.

Just like Hasenkrug and Marieke, Büttner skimmed through the client file, then whistled through his teeth. "Well, there are quite a few acquaintances who present themselves to the outside world as clean and caring family men. I can imagine that some of them are having a restless night's sleep right now."

Marieke snorted. "Serves them right. And I hope their restless sleep will be the least of their problems for the foreseeable future."

"Maybe they didn't know that the women were not participating voluntarily," Hasenkrug said. "Watching pornography is not a crime per se.

"They will get mail from the public prosecutor's office," Marieke replied. "And it would be enough for me if their wives or girlfriends got hold of it and maybe even read it."

Hasenkrug played in the list of young women. There were eleven in total, among them Julia Vogler.

Büttner stumbled as his gaze lingered on one of the first names. At the same moment, Hasenkrug made a surprised sound and said: "Sanna. Well, the name is not that common. Now someone would just have to use the video to verify whether …"

Büttner waved it off. "Not me." As long as it could be avoided, he wanted nothing more to do with the videos.

"Do you have the files?" asked Marieke.

"Yeah, sure."

"Then send Sanna's to my mobile phone. And Lisa's, too, because I have a fear."

"The women whose surnames are also given are the ones already identified by our colleagues, I assume?" inquired Büttner, while unambiguous sounds could be heard from his colleague's smartphone. "Could you please turn off the sound, Marieke?!"

"Yes, they are identified," Hasenkrug confirmed. He tapped away on his keyboard, then raised his eyebrows in amazement. "Well, look at that!"

"It's definitely Sanna and Lisa from the riding school," Marieke confirmed her suspicions the next moment. "It looks like Jesko has been poaching there quite a bit. Gina, Lisa and Sanna. His haul is quite impressive. He really fucked his way through the riding school. So we should definitely have another look around there. It's possible that there are more of Jesko's porn victims going in and out of the stud farm."

Büttner nodded at her before turning back to his assistant. "What have you discovered, Hasenkrug?"

"A building block to what Marieke just mentioned. Silvia Remmers. She is the riding therapist who works at the equestrian centre."

"What?!" Marieke looked at him with wide eyes. "But I can't imagine … can you send me the corresponding video, Sebastian? After all, there are many women named Silvia Remmers in East Frisia and …" She opened the video and sucked in a sharp breath. "Okay, it's her. Crap. I'd better turn it off right away, because after all, I don't want to have this video in front of my eyes all the time during my next therapy sessions." She shook her head as if she wanted to catapult the images she had seen right back out of it.

"We will have to confront the women with these recordings willy-nilly," Büttner remarked. "It can be assumed that they are just as clueless as Julia Vogler. So this is not going to be fun."

"If Jesko Mudder were our murder victim, we would now have a whole series of suspects with motive," Marieke stated. "But why did Gina have to die? So far – porn or no porn – that makes no sense."

"By the way, a corresponding video was also recorded by Gina," Hasenkrug reported. "Jesko just hadn't uploaded it yet. But he had already found a fake name for her: Alma."

"At least Gina has been spared a lot in that respect," Büttner noted. He sighed, "but unfortunately that doesn't help her anymore." He paused for a moment and looked off into nowhere, brooding. "Do we also have the video of Gina?" he then asked.

"Yes, why?"

"Is she wearing the necklace on it that was mentioned earlier?"

"You mean, is it possible that the video was taken just before she died?"

Büttner nodded.

Hasenkrug played the video on the monitor and was about to start it when Büttner stopped him. "It's really not necessary for all of us to watch it. That would be too disrespectful for me. Take a look, Hasenkrug, and then just tell us whether the necklace can be seen or not."

"She is," Hasenkrug said a little later. She also keeps them during … so …" He cleared his throat. "Well, she wears them."

"Then we can probably assume that the video was taken between the visit to her parents and her full bath," Büttner said. "That's also the reason why it hasn't been uploaded yet."

"And we know that Jesko was also with her in his flat at least until shortly before the murder," Marieke added. "That definitely makes him a possible perpetrator."

"So far, so good." Büttner looked at Marieke, who was

sitting there with a contracted brow. "But you also wanted to say something earlier, if I remember correctly."

Marieke yawned. "Sorry, but I realise that I am not yet as resilient as I would like to be. I'll probably have to rest again in a minute. But quickly to what I wanted to say before Sebastian barged in on me with his porn. I don't know if you know it yet, but you talked to Christopher Grensemann, didn't you?"

"We did," Hasenkrug confirmed. "He seems to be Sanna's current lover. Did you have any dealings with him at the riding school?"

"Not yet. I've only seen him walking around there. I said hello when I rode past him. But he didn't pay any attention to me at all. He doesn't seem to have any interest in physically impaired people. Not sexy enough."

Büttner gasped indignantly. "This just gets better and better! But that's exactly how I assessed this guy. He is …"

Marieke stopped him with a gesture. "It's cool if he doesn't pay attention to me, boss. That way he certainly won't suspect me of snooping around after him either. If only because, in case of doubt, he already doesn't know I exist."

"And what is so exciting to report about him now?", Hasenkrug wanted to know.

"Let's see the next photo."

Within minutes, this appeared on the screen. It showed two young men arm in arm, and quite obviously after a horse show, because one of them – Büttner recognised him as Christopher Grensemann, who was a few years younger – was not only wearing riding clothes including a helmet, but was also holding up one of those gold-coloured ribbons that you get after winning a show. The other man was Jesko Mudder.

"They know each other?" he wondered.

"Yes. From primary school. They are the same age. Both twenty-three. Except that Christopher has A-levels, while Jesko completed secondary school and then did his apprenticeship as a motor vehicle mechatronics technician."

"And to what extent is that interesting for us?" asked Hasenkrug.

"I don't know yet. But I intend to find out. Especially since there are more interesting things to report."

"Namely?"

"Holger Moersler. He is the third in the group. I don't know how close he is to Jesko and Christopher today. But when they were at primary school, the three of them supposedly formed an inseparable trio. That's why I wonder, among other things, why Kira Grensemann claimed to hardly know Jesko." Marieke yawned again. "Sorry, but I really need to take a break before I go to the riding school again later. I've arranged another therapy session with Silvia and I'll take the opportunity to find out a bit about the friendship between the men. From what I hear, at least Jesko and Christopher are still quite thick with each other."

"It would be interesting to know if Christopher knew about this porn thing," Hasenkrug said. "Maybe he was in on it with Jesko."

"When it comes to picking up women, one of them is in no way inferior to the other, that much I have already found out," Marieke replied. "What Holger Moersler has to do with women, and if he has any, I don't know yet. Anyway, I would have a lot of fun searching the Grensemanns' house. But I'm afraid we don't have enough information for that yet, do we?"

Büttner nodded. "Not by a long shot. But maybe things will look different soon after you've asked around there a bit." He raised his index finger admonishingly. "Asked around, not looked around!"

Marieke shrugged regretfully. She reached for her crutches and, leaning on them, heaved herself up from the chair. "Unfortunately, your reminder won't come to nothing this time boss, because I'm not mobile enough to look around again yet." She lifted one of the crutches and flashed a wry grin. "Because walking on four legs isn't half as good as walking on two. Strange, isn't it?"

Which was unfortunate, Büttner thought, because Marieke's notorious solo efforts had often brought them important insights. But of course, he would never say that out loud.

"Very well," he bid her farewell. "Then I wish you good luck with your research at the equestrian farm. But take care of yourself! Murderers are not generally to be trifled with when they feel cornered."

"We don't even know if there's a murderer running around yet!" Marieke shouted back over her shoulder.

"He or she has to be somewhere. So why not there?" murmured Büttner.

13

Holger Moersler did not show up for work that day, as David Büttner and Sebastian Hasenkrug found out when they visited the horse farm again.

"He's taking care of his mother," Kira Grensemann explained to them while leading a horse by the reins and walking in circles, at a rather leisurely pace. On the horse's back sat an elderly woman who, even Büttner noticed, was completely tense. It almost seemed as if she was afraid of riding. But then why was she doing it?

"Why don't you loosen up, Hanne!" Kira Grensemann called out to her with a slightly annoyed undertone. "How is the horse supposed to stay relaxed if you're not?! And keep your back straight, even a sack of oats cuts a more elegant figure than you!"

That was not very friendly, Büttner thought. Especially since the rider was a customer. But maybe she hadn't even heard it, the way she was staring and pinching herself. "Is there a reason why she is torturing herself like this?

"She says she finally wants to prove to everyone that she can do it."

"Who is everyone?"

"I have no idea. It seems to be about overcoming a childhood trauma if I understood her correctly. She wouldn't give me any more details. But I guess I'll have to tell her that there's no point. It is already her fourth lesson; but instead of becoming more relaxed, she is getting more and more tense. If it goes on like this, she'll have another panic attack up there. And look at that poor horse! Aurora is the gentlest creature there is on this stud farm and far beyond. But you can see how nervous even she is. I've never seen the animal so stressed."

"What's wrong with Moersler's mother that he can't come to work because of her?", Hasenkrug brought the conversation back to the house and stable master. The next moment, however, he put a hand over his eyes and peered through his fingers at the rider, who was now making an effort to claw her hands and the reins into Aurora's mane. "Oh dear, I can't bear to watch that."

"Okay, Hanne, that's it for today!" shouted Kira Grensemann as the horse began to prance restlessly – which in turn caused the rider to let out a strangled cry. "That's not the way to do it! This is not how it goes at all!" She beckoned an older man in jeans and a flannel shirt, who had been standing there leaning against the wall with his arms folded for a few minutes, shaking his head every now and then. Apparently, he couldn't believe the incompetence he was being offered here either. "You help Hanne dismount," she asked him as he immediately stood next to the boss, who pressed the lunge into his hand. "Tell her to go to my office and wait for me. I'll talk her out of the idea of riding as soon as I'm done here."

"Better is," the man growled. "No one can stand the way that woman makes Aurora crazy."

"Holger's mother is terminally ill. She has ALS and has been bedridden for a few weeks," Kira Grensemann answered Hasenkrug's question. "Yet she is only in her early fifties. Holger's grandmother tries to take care of her as best she can, but she is already over eighty and is hopelessly overwhelmed by the care of her daughter.

Of course she was. Büttner sighed inwardly. A mother over eighty who nursed her daughter to death. What a shitty fate! At a miserable croak from Hanne, he looked over at the horse and rider again. Was he imagining it, or did the mare actually look relieved after Hanne had slipped off her back in a daring manoeuvre more than she had climbed?

"Have your son and Sanna actually been a couple for a long time?" inquired Hasenkrug as the two young people rode out through the barn door not far from them. After several days of continuous rain, it was dry today and even the sun peeked out from time to time between the clouds. The wind had also died down considerably.

Kira Grensemann made an inarticulate sound before she said, "What does couple mean? I'm afraid that term doesn't appear in my son's vocabulary. He does it the way he likes it. Here today, there tomorrow. Friendship plus is what they call it nowadays. I don't even want to know how many girls and women he has broken the hearts of." It didn't sound as if she had much sympathy for her son in this respect.

"They say similar things about Jesko Mudder," Büttner remarked, hoping she would jump on it.

She did. "Yes. Sometimes I think that the two of them have arranged some kind of competition. Along the lines of who can get the most women into bed. It's certainly not about the girls' feelings." She looked thoughtfully after the two riders who were slowly riding along the country lane. "I just always wonder why the girls let it happen to them. They should have realised by now what's going on."

"Do Jesko and Christopher know each other well?" asked Hasenkrug.

"Yes, for a very long time," Kira Grensemann confirmed what Marieke had already found out.

"Yet you recently claimed not to know him well."

"Just because you've known a person for a long time doesn't mean you really know him," Kira Grensemann dismissed the objection. "And I can't say that Jesko has been a good influence on Christopher," she sighed resignedly as she again beat her riding crop rhythmically against her lower leg. "I had fears to that effect early on. Jesko always had stupid things on his mind even as a child and was not very nice to his fellow men. They were still in primary school then. But unfortunately I didn't succeed in keeping Christopher away from Jesko by any means. The two of them always got back together, no matter what other contact they had. I couldn't count on my partner at the time, Christopher's biological father, because he preferred to hang around in pubs rather than take an interest in his son's affairs. At some point I gave up."

"Even the women seemed to enjoy leaving them to each other," Büttner put it in a deliberately provocative way.

"As I said, the women get involved. What can you do?"

"Despite this knowledge, you let Christopher and Jesko poach unhindered in your riding stable."

The riding instructor shrugged her shoulders. "I can't

very well forbid my son access to the stables. And the girls … well, they are of age and have to learn their lessons themselves."

"Yes, and in a pretty harsh way," Büttner replied.

"What do you mean?" Kira Grensemann looked at him suspiciously. "You're not suggesting Christopher had anything to do with Gina's death, are you?" She laughed bitterly. "In that case, you'd better stick to Jesko, after all, Gina was with him."

"You don't necessarily have to be with someone to kill them," Büttner countered. "If it were, we wouldn't have a particularly demanding job."

"Christopher had nothing to do with Gina's death."

"And you know that so well because …?"

"I do know my son! Yes, Christopher has slipped away from me a little due to Jesko's influence. And yes, he is a little too smug and arrogant in many places, which – by the way – he gets from his father. I'm aware of all that, and I don't want to defend him at all. But he is not a murderer. Full stop."

"We'll get to the point in due time, Mrs Grensemann," Büttner replied, unimpressed. "It's still a little too early for that, don't you think?" He focused on two women who came in the stable gate. They waved at the stud manager. But no sooner did they realise who was standing with her than they turned on their heels and hurried back out.

"That was Tomke and Lisa," Hasenkrug stated, and he nodded meaningfully at Büttner.

Büttner looked at his wristwatch in amazement. "Shouldn't they be at school or work at this time? And Sanna too?"

"You … well." Kira Grensemann cleared her throat. "They do one job or another after they … graduate from school until they decide what they want to do with their lives. They also help out here with us on a regular basis. I called them this morning and asked them to come when it was clear that Holger wouldn't be here. After all, you can't do without help."

"And Silvia Remmers, the therapist, is she here?" inquired Hasenkrug. "We would have to talk to her, too."

"You want to talk to Silvia? May I ask what she has to do with all this?"

"You may. Well? Is she there?"

"I see." Kira Grensemann scowled at him. "No. Silvia won't be here until the afternoon."

"Then we'd like her address." When the farm owner hesitated, Büttner added: "We'll find out anyway. It would just be quicker if we got it from you. Or is there a reason why you don't want to hand them over? Well, we'll find that out in time, too." He didn't feel like being stalled by anyone.

"Good." She dictated the address to Hasenkrug in the notepad.

"Oh, that was a short ride," he said as Sanna and Christopher rode back into the yard. They got off their horses and led them towards the stables.

"One of the horses had twisted its leg a few days ago while riding out in the open," Kira Grensemann explained. "They just wanted to see if it was resilient again." Her smartphone started ringing and she pulled it out of the pocket of her waistcoat. After a glance at the display, which caused her to frown, she suddenly looked nervous. "Is that it now?" she asked impatiently. "I'd have to answer that. You'll find Holger, as I said, at his mother's." She didn't wait for an answer, but took the call with a curt "Yes" as she moved away with quick steps.

"Well," said Büttner, who was anything but comfortable with their upcoming mission, "now that Sanna and Lisa are here, we'll take the opportunity to confront them with the videos."

"I wonder why Tomke isn't on these videos," Hasenkrug said as they walked side by side to the pit stall. "She is no less pretty than the others, but Jesko doesn't have her in his porn pool yet, as we know."

"Maybe she is the only one who has seen what is going on here," Büttner reflected. "Which would be unfortunate, as the others will now have to painfully learn." He stretched his face towards the sun, which was flashing through the clouds at that moment. He could barely remember the last time he had seen it, let alone felt it on his skin. Nor could he remember ever having experienced such a thoroughly gloomy and wet November, although even under normal circumstances it wasn't exactly known as a merry month.

As yesterday, they met Lisa and Tomke in two of the horse stalls. Büttner, feeling Tomke's sceptical gaze at his back, approached the stall where Lisa was standing, working the coat of a brown horse with a brush in strokes that were as rough as they were strong. "Lisa?" he addressed her. He almost expected her not to answer again because of her headphones, but she turned to him with a "Huh?". When she realised who was standing in front of her, her facial expression changed and she looked over at her friend in search of help. She shrugged her shoulders and went back to cleaning out a box. "What else is there?" Lisa was obviously trying to keep her voice firm, but she was not succeeding.

"You don't happen to know where Sanna is, do you?" Hasenkrug turned to Lisa before Büttner could answer her. He looked around searchingly, but like his boss, he couldn't spot her anywhere. "We'd like to talk to you together."

"She … uh … I don't know. Haven't seen her yet today. I don't think she's here."

Büttner was pretty sure she was lying, because they had actually met on the dirt road.

"Yes, she is. We just saw her. With Christopher." Hasenkrug made his way to the free run and returned only a little later with Sanna in tow. "Is there somewhere we can talk undisturbed?"

"About what?" Sanna took off her riding helmet and shook out her red curls.

"We'll tell you then. Well?"

"We could go to the Reiterstübchen." At the questioning look of the commissioners, she added: "Above the stands. That's where the guests at the tournaments can have a coffee and stuff."

"Sounds like a good plan." Büttner would also have liked a coffee now, but he doubted he would be offered one.

A few minutes later, they entered the room from which they had a good view of the riding hall. The front of the room was completely glazed, and the individual elements could be moved in such a way that the room virtually became a balcony. Apparently, a fair amount of money had been spent here to make the guests' stay as pleasant as possible at any time of the year.

The room itself had a solid wooden counter, behind which stretched a wall of shelves perhaps four metres long. On it were dozens of cups and pennants lined up, as well as lots of cups and glasses.

In front of the bar were a total of six round tables, each with four chairs. They took a seat at one of the tables.

"We would like to show you something," Büttner got straight to the point. "And please tell us if you had any knowledge of it." With a movement of his head, he asked Hasenkrug to show the women Jesko's website where the porn videos had been shown.

Hasenkrug initially refrained from playing the video sequences, but only showed them the picture Jesko had set as an eye-catcher for his customers.

Lisa raised her eyes in horror after recognising herself in the picture. "A-but … where did you get that?" She swallowed dryly. "And … and what do you see when you click on it?"

It was also easy to see from Sanna's reaction that these two women, just like Julia Vogler, had known nothing about the porn site.

"This is a website run by Jesko Mudder," Hasenkrug explained. "A paid site," he added.

"Th-that means he filmed us and d-then … d-then as porn …" Lisa couldn't finish the sentence because she was so shocked.

Hasenkrug nodded. "That's exactly how it is. The site has been running for just over a year and has several hundred hits a day."

"Oh, my God." Lisa put her hands in front of her face and began to sob.

"Th-that pig," Sanna gasped, having regained her speech. Her freckled face was as white as the whitewashed wall behind her. "T-that can't be what he did … I mean … he couldn't have really done that."

"You should file a complaint," Büttner advised them, to which the two merely nodded lamely. "For that, you would have to come by our office as soon as possible.

Another nod followed, but Büttner was not sure if they had actually understood him.

"Is … is the site still on the net?" asked Sanna.

"No. It was switched off by the public prosecutor's office," Büttner reassured her. "But I think now you understand why we are so urgently looking for Jesko Mudder. I assume the APBs have not passed you by. So if you know where he is, please tell us now."

Sanna and Lisa glanced at each other, then both shook their heads silently.

"We … we don't know," Sanna said. "And believe me, after this …" she made a snide gesture towards Hasenkrug's mobile phone, "we'd rather blow the whistle on him sooner rather than later. Wouldn't we, Lisa?"

She nodded while tears ran down her cheeks.

"Is your friend here somewhere?" asked Büttner. "We urgently need to speak to him, too."

Sanna opened her eyes in shock. "Did Christopher have something to do with it?"

"You mean with the videos?", Büttner made sure.

"Yes."

"So far there are no indications of this. But of course we can't rule it out either. From what we've heard, Jesko and Christopher are close friends, so …" He let the rest of the sentence hang meaningfully in the air.

"I'll give him hell," Sanna clenched her teeth. "I swear I'll crush him with my own hands."

"As I said, we don't know if he knew about the site. The best thing will probably be for you to ask him about it."

"Of course he knew about it," Sanna sneered, suddenly awakening from her state of shock. "Jesko and Christopher know every fucking thing about each other. So it's hard to imagine that Jesko of all people did this on his own, isn't it?"

Büttner refrained from answering. He had achieved what he wanted to achieve. Maybe the women would come to their senses after all and finally say what they knew about Gina without feeling that they were betraying someone's trust. Because whose trust had been betrayed by whom should have become clear to them by now at the latest.

14

"You'd almost think our witnesses had agreed to make Jesko Mudder look like a bad person and thus the main suspect in our murder case," said Sebastian Hasenkrug as they made their way from the horse farm to tranquil Groothusen to pay Holger Moersler a visit. "I would bet that Moersler will also be blowing the same horn."

"Jesko Mudder *is* a bad person," David Büttner replied. "And that's regardless of whether he killed Gina or not. Or what would you call a man who exploits his sexual relationships with women so shamelessly and turns them into money in a disgusting way?"

"Of course, I agree. Nevertheless, all the witnesses seem to be eager for us to focus on him as well, as far as the murder is concerned."

"Maybe because they really believe he's Gina's killer."

Hasenkrug did not seem convinced. "No, there is something else. Something doesn't fit there. I just can't grasp it yet."

"Then let me know as soon as you get hold of it. For now, we'll take care of this Holger Moser."

"Moersler."

"About that one, too, for all I care." Büttner steered his vehicle into the paved driveway. Moersler and his mother lived in a two-storey single-family house made of red clinker brick and with a peaked roof, like thousands of others in East Frisia. He stopped in front of the garage, where the grey overhead door was half open. Büttner estimated that the house had been built in the fifties, like all the other houses in this street that were built in a very similar style. It was unadorned, just like the front garden, which consisted of nothing but a lawn overgrown with moss. Yellowed curtains hung in front of the three equally sized gable windows, and largely withered green plants stood on the interior windowsills. All in all, the property made a desolate, almost abandoned impression.

"I guess it's one of those houses that a post-war couple saved from their mouths so that their children would have it better one day," Hasenkrug remarked. He bent down and peered under the tilted door into the garage. "Wow, Moersler rides a motorbike," he noted. "A pretty impressive bike. Respect, such a thing has to be earned first!"

"There's no car?" asked Büttner, who didn't feel like bending down to inspect the garage as well.

"Yes, there is. An older Fiat. Not nearly as spectacular as the motorbike. Maybe it's the mothers."

"Anything else of interest?"

"Not at first glance, no. But not much else fits in here either."

"Very well." Büttner pressed the bell button. Immediately, shuffling footsteps could be heard from the house, then the door was opened. In front of them stood a not at all unattractive young man in his thirties. With his athletic build, angular features and three-day beard, he was a match for Jesko and Christopher, at least visually. An obviously freshly lit cigarette was stuck in the corner of his mouth, its blue haze wafting around his face, and he looked at her from narrowed eyes. "Moin. If you're from Jehovah's Witnesses and want to tell me about the imminent demise of the world, you can leave right now."

"We were lucky again." Büttner pulled out his service card and introduced himself and Hasenkrug. "We are here because of the Gina Gloger murder case and would like to talk to you."

Moersler's gaze became suspicious, but Büttner thought he saw a hint of sadness when Gina's name was mentioned. He took a drag of his cigarette, then carelessly flicked the ash in front of the door so that it came to rest on the top of the three steps of the outside staircase, which was immediately blown away by a gust of wind. "Who sent you here?"

Büttner raised his brows. "Sent here?"

"Well, you must know from someone that Gina and I … that we know each other." He contorted his face as if in sudden pain. "Knew each other," he then added much more quietly.

"We were at the Grensemanns' horse farm," Hasenkrug said. "Your name came up there. We were told that you were not coming to work at the moment because you were looking after your mother."

"Yes." He took a deep drag of his cigarette, put his head back and blew out the smoke. "She's getting worse every day. I don't want to leave her alone."

"Understandable." Büttner looked towards the street. On the pavement, an elderly woman with a walker had stopped and was looking over at them. "Oh dear," she exclaimed in a raspy voice, "I guess it's happened now! You must be from the funeral home, aren't you?"

Holger Moersler winced briefly, then called back in a cutting voice: "Why do you want to know that, Hertha, hey? Or have you decided to finally make your exit? Then I'll gladly send the gentlemen over to you!"

"But …"

He made a movement as if to shoo away an annoying insect. "Get on with it, Hertha! There's nothing here for you vultures yet!"

"What in the world was that?!" asked Büttner, horrified, as the woman now went on her way with tippy-toe steps.

Moersler snorted disparagingly. "The dear neighbours pretend to be interested in my mother's fate. But they're just eager to finally have something to gossip about. And everyone wants to be the first to break the news." He looked at Büttner out of sad eyes. "Believe me, in a situation like this you find out who is friend and who is foe. My mother has spent her whole life in this village, so you would think there would be more support. Especially from those who knew her as a child. But I guess our world doesn't work like that anymore."

"Perhaps we should rather continue our conversation indoors so as not to give the neighbours cause for more gossip," Büttner suggested.

Moersler dropped his half-smoked cigarette on the floor and kicked it out with the heel of his shoe, then blew the smoke out through his nose and gestured for them to come in.

"We can sit in the kitchen," he said, holding open a door. "Go on in. I'll make us some tea in a minute. But first I want to check on my mother in the living room for a moment."

Büttner and Hasenkrug took seats on chairs at a somewhat wobbly-looking table so as not to have to squeeze between the table and the East Frisian sofa. Büttner let his gaze wander through the kitchen. The built-in cupboards had been modern in the eighties, yellowed Prill flowers stuck to the tiles. The wallpaper and the paint on the walls around the kitchen counter, however, looked as if they had been freshly applied not so long ago. Holes had burnt into the beige-patterned PVC floor, presumably from the odd dropped cigarette. All in all, the kitchen did not look modern, but tidy and clean.

"All this is still from my grandparents," explained Holger Moersler, who came through the door as if he had to apologise for the set-up. "My mother raised me alone, so she only worked part-time, so there weren't any big jumps in it." He sighed. "I used to give her a hard time about that because almost all my friends had more useless stuff than me. Just the way teenagers are. Today I feel differently about it. She gave up so much for me." He picked up a pencil with an eraser lying on the table and bounced it up and down on the stained tabletop. "Let's face it, what good is the biggest and finest mansion if love and understanding are lacking? And my mother gave me plenty of that." He wiped his eyes bashfully. "I really wish I had been more grateful. And most of all, I wish I had spent more time with her. It would have brought her joy. Now it's too late." He looked at Buettner. "You know she has terminal ALS?"

Büttner swallowed a lump that had formed in his throat after this short but emotional monologue, and he nodded when their eyes met. He didn't know who exactly he had expected to meet here, but certainly not a young man as reflective and empathetic as this. "You're here for your mother now," he said after a brief pause. "That is more than many others get to experience."

"Sure." Moersler stroked his forehead with his fingers as if he suddenly had a headache. "But, as I said, it's too late. The doctor says she only has a few days left. If at all. It's not fair."

"It rarely is," Büttner murmured.

Moersler filled water into a kettle and put it on the cooker. "You'll have some tea, won't you?"

"Please. Thank you."

Büttner was grateful when Hasenkrug now brought the subject up about her murder case. "Without beating about the bush, Mr Moersler," Hasenkrug said, "at the equestrian centre we were told that you were in love with Gina. Is that right?"

"No." Moersler scooped tea leaves into a stainless-steel kettle.

"No?"

"No. I wasn't in love with her. I loved her." He took three cups and a bowl of sugar cubes from the cupboard and placed them on the table. His expression was suddenly frozen.

"Oh."

"And she loved me. But probably no one told you that."

The kettle began to whistle. Moersler took it off the cooker and poured boiling hot water over the tea leaves.

"Uh… no." Büttner did not yet know how to classify this new information.

"They probably told you that Gina didn't want to know anything about me. But the fact is that I didn't want to put her through all this," Moersler made an expansive movement with his right arm.

"That means Gina wanted to be with you?"

Moersler nodded. "We both wanted it. But, as I said … It wouldn't have been fair to tie her to me and thus to this situation. I wanted Gina to be free and not feel obligated to me or even my mother to do anything." He put cubes in the cups with tongs. As he poured the hot tea over them, they crackled. "Cream?" he asked.

"Uh… no, thanks." Büttner stared at his steaming tea as if he could find the truth in it. He didn't know what to make of Moersler's words. However, he did not at all give the impression that he was telling them some made-up story. But that didn't mean he wasn't, as Büttner knew from many years of experience. Perhaps Moersler had only rehearsed this number well because he knew that sooner or later they would turn up at his place.

"If Gina loved you," Hasenkrug hammered out, "why was she with Jesko Mudder?"

Moersler let out a bitter laugh. "Gina wouldn't accept me sending her away. There was a huge fuss, she cried, screamed, begged me. When I maintained that this was not the right time for me or for her to plunge into a love adventure, she said nothing more for minutes. But then she hissed at me that I'll see what I get out of it and left, slamming the door. Only two days later I heard that she had thrown herself at Jesko." He pressed his lips together and looked sadly out the window, against which the autumn rain was once again pelting. "Jesko, of all people. She really knew how to hurt me the most. And now …" He made a jittery gesture with his hand. When he lifted his gaze, his eyes were swimming in tears. "She would still be alive if I hadn't sent her away, wouldn't she?"

"That … uh … is pure speculation." Büttner felt overwhelmed by the situation. When Hasenkrug said nothing either, he sipped his tea to gain time. "Do you have any suspicions about who might have killed Gina?" he asked after a long silence.

"No. I absolutely cannot imagine who could have done it."

Büttner waited for a but followed by Jesko's name, but Moersler remained silent. This made him the first not to voice this suspicion – although he would probably have had the most plausible reason to make such an accusation. All the others had voiced this suspicion even before they knew about the porn and thus had every reason to be angry with Jesko Mudder.

"As we heard, you used to be close friends with Jesko. And also with Christopher Grensemann," Hasenkrug also found his language again. "Why aren't you friends anymore?"

"Because Jesko mutated into an asshole a long time ago," Moersler answered without hesitation.

Well, this formulation left little room for interpretation.

"I thought it was just a phase at first," Moersler continued. He had not sipped his tea once, merely stirred it listlessly with a spoon. "But if it is a phase, it will last until today. I don't want anything more to do with Jesko."

Then it seemed only logical – assuming Moersler's story was true – that Gina had attached herself to him, of all people, to spite the man she really loved. But what did all this have to do with the murder?

"You had an argument with Jesko recently, we heard."

"You must mean Kira's birthday party." He sighed as tears ran down his cheek, making no effort to hide them from them. "I had been drinking, Jesko provoked me. He was treating Gina like one of his sluts that he keeps picking up randomly. I really tried to restrain myself but he wouldn't stop. So I gonged him a few. Then there was silence."

"We checked," Hasenkrug said. "He didn't press charges against you. Can you tell us why he waived it?"

"Nah, you'll have to ask him that yourself. But it's quite possible that he knows himself that he's an obnoxious asshole. Somewhere deep inside him."

If Jesko merely knew it deep inside, then things would be worse for him than Büttner had assumed so far. Jesko was certainly aware that what he was doing to the young women was not only a character flaw, but criminal in the extreme. A more disgusting asshole than Mudder could possibly be. It was just a pity that he still hadn't been found. Büttner would have been only too happy to put him through the wringer.

"You ride a cool motorbike," Hasenkrug said, whereupon Büttner looked at him in amazement. Did his assistant really think that now was the right time to steer the conversation towards more innocuous topics?

"It's my mother's."

"What?" Hasenkrug leaned forward as if he hadn't understood properly.

"My mother is the cool sock in this house, not me." Moersler smiled. "She saved her whole life for this machine. Then three years ago she was finally able to fulfil her big dream." The smile on his face gave way to a shadow. "She didn't have it for long, but I'm grateful that I was able to do my part to help her live her dream for at least a little while longer."

"That means you supported the purchase financially?" Büttner could not imagine that a caretaker's salary allowed such expenditure.

"I was still working as an IT person at the time and making lots of money."

"Oh?" Büttner looked around the kitchen and promptly felt caught when Moersler said, "My mother never wanted me to help her financially. Her pride wouldn't allow it. Only in the case of the motorbike did she accept it, albeit under protest." His expression became thoughtful. "Today I think she may have known back then that she wouldn't have time to get every last cent of the money together on her own."

"Why did you leave your job?"

"Because Kira offered me the other one. She knew about our situation and wanted to help. This gives me the flexibility I need. My other job wouldn't have given me that."

Hasenkrug's mobile beeped, which seemed inappropriately loud to Büttner given the silence that had developed in the room.

"Oh," escaped his assistant when he read the message, and the very next moment he pressed the phone into his hand so that his boss could also read the message he had received.

"Oh," it now escaped Büttner as well. He cleared his throat before placing his business card on the table and saying, "We have to go again, Mr Moersler. Thank you for taking the time to talk to us."

Holger Moersler only nodded, then accompanied them to the door. "Please, find the pig that took Gina from me," he gave them as a farewell.

Büttner nodded at him. "All the best to you."

15

Before David Büttner started the car, he glanced at his smartphone. A glow crossed his face when a message from Jette was announced. He called her up.

It's so beautiful here, Pops, even you would like it.

This was probably an allusion to the fact that he didn't think much of travel in general and long-distance travel in particular, and considered the sofa at home to be much more relaxing than the sun, beach and sea.

Debbie and I walked down to the promenade very early in the morning. The sunrise was like something from another world.

"I don't want to push, boss," Hasenkrug said.

"Then just leave it," Büttner replied absently.

Here in Sea Point there is a swimming pool right by the sea. It's absolutely amazing.

"Well, I just thought that the discovery of the body in Greetsiel might be of superficial interest."

After our English lesson, Debbie and I are going for a walk along the coast. Towards Clifton and Camps Beach. I am so happy to be here.

"The nice thing about corpses is that they don't run away, Hasenkrug. Which should apply to the new corpse in Greetsiel no less than to all the others that have been laid at our feet over time."

Büttner did not let himself be distracted, but scrolled through the photos by means of which Jette tried to support her enthusiasm. And, he had to admit, she was right, because the beauty of the landscape at the Cape aroused a feeling of longing even in him. And Debbie – Büttner estimated her to be in her sixties – who was beaming in a selfie with Jette and the sunrise, really made a thoroughly likeable impression.

"Take a look at this, Hasenkrug." He pressed his smartphone into the hand of his assistant, who sighed in surrender. "I think Jette hit it pretty well."

"Well, that might be the understatement of the century," Hasenkrug said, nodding impressively after looking at the photos. He handed the phone back to his boss. "I have no small desire to get on the next plane to Cape Town."

Büttner let his gaze wander through the rain-soaked windscreen along the dull grey street. Even the otherwise friendly red of the houses looked washed out, not to mention the desolate plants in the gardens and the bare branches of the trees. He didn't feel like getting on a plane to anywhere, but a little sun would be nice.

"Well then, let's go and see who has been caught by the fishermen." He started the engine and backed the car up, then drove towards Greetsiel. Hasenkrug had received news that the Greetsielers had fished a corpse out of the North Sea as a by-catch to the crabs; which would probably be quite an unappetising sight – and not only for those who had been looking forward to a tasty crab roll. But whether this corpse had anything to do with her case was written in the stars. Büttner hoped so, because having to deal with yet another murder case was not exactly what he was looking for.

The Greetsiel cutter harbour was already widely cordoned off. So, the colleagues had learned from their mistakes. Which became a problem for Büttner and Hasenkrug at the moment, when a young policeman in uniform told them in the centre of the village, with somewhat clumsy arm movements, to turn their vehicle around and drive back in the direction from which they had come.

Büttner stopped and lowered the window. The rain promptly hit him cold in the face. Before he could say anything, the young colleague snapped at him in an imperious tone: "What exactly did you not understand about my gestures?"

"Moin. If I'm honest, quite a lot," Büttner replied calmly. "You can certainly do better than that, don't you think?"

He looked at Hasenkrug, who winked at him in amusement.

"Now don't get rude!"

Büttner sighed. "Believe me, I only mean well with you. Although I can't say I particularly like your tone. Do you always snap at people like that?"

The young, uniformed man looked irritated for a moment. His mission was probably not going as he had imagined. He pointed to the red and white flagging tape stretched across the red-paved street, which, set in vibration by the wind, made buzzing noises. "As you can see, this is a police operation!"

"Now you're just saying."

"Can't you see you're holding up all the traffic here?!

The driver behind you is already getting restless. So, turn around now, or I'll have to … uh… issue a warning."

"So, you must." Büttner glanced in the rear-view mirror. There was another car behind him, but the next moment it started to turn. There was no sign of agitation or even annoyance on the part of the driver. As another vehicle approached from behind, he took pity on his colleague, who was probably a trainee and was nervously hopping from one leg to the other. He assumed that he had been placed at this post despite his obvious inexperience because the more experienced colleagues did not feel like directing traffic in the rain.

Büttner's renitence seemed to be getting to the young policeman, for he chewed helplessly on his lower lip and seemed to be thinking about what the next step might be, according to the police manual.

Büttner, for his part, waited patiently.

"Driving licence and vehicle registration please," the uniformed man finally pressed out helplessly.

Büttner decided to put an end to the spook and held out his service card to him. "I think this one will do."

No sooner had the young man realised who he was dealing with, when his complexion changed from red to pale, and it was impossible not to notice that he would have loved to have plunged into the next hole and dug his way all the way to Australia. "Uh… uh… well, Mr… uh… Chief Inspector, I would like to apologise that …"

"That's very kind of you," Büttner interrupted the stammering. "But I would be satisfied if you could finally clear the way for us."

"N-naturally. G-with pleasure." The unlucky worm hurried to lift the flutter tape so that Büttner could drive his car under it.

"Thank you," Büttner said simply, then continued on his way towards the harbour.

"That wasn't very nice of you, boss." Hasenkrug grinned broadly. "The poor guy will …"

"… get over it," Büttner added. "If not, he should think about a new profession. He's lucky I'm such a patient person."

"You paraded him."

Büttner raised his index finger. "But with patience."

In contrast to last time, there were only a few people at the cutter harbour today, so Büttner drove right up to the harbour wall. There he parked the car and they walked towards the rocking cutters, which were bustling with people. It seemed that it had not been long since the fleet had arrived, and now men and women dressed in oilskins were unloading the catch packed in boxes on almost all the cutters. Only on one of the cutters, which lay at the very front of the quay, was it exceptionally quiet, but a number of people had gathered in front of it. Among them was Dr Anja Wilkens, who was bent over a body covered with a plastic tarpaulin, risking a glance under the tarpaulin and lowering it again quite quickly with a pained expression on her face.

"Nothing you want to smell," she said to Büttner as he now stood next to her. "You'd better look at the photos later. It's not a pretty sight either, but it'll do without the acrid smell. Hi, David."

"Hello, Anja. Can you still tell who it is?"

"Jesko Mudder," growled a fisherman. He stood, hands buried deep in the pockets of his orange oil jacket, very close to her. "Doesn't look very good anymore, if you ask me. And it doesn't smell good either." He shrugged his shoulders. "But what are you going to do when you end up in a net among crabs. You can't win any beauty prizes with that."

"I don't know about you, Commissioner, but I wonder what he was doing out there," said another man in oilskins. "He wasn't fishing, I'd say."

"Yes, I am inclined to agree with that conclusion," Büttner assured him. The irony in his voice seemed to escape the fisherman, however, because he nodded with a sigh. "Not nice, that."

"Jo, tell me about it," the other agreed with him.

"Jo, tell me about it," echoed Büttner, whereupon the corner of Hasenkrug's mouth twitched telltale.

Büttner thoughtfully kept his gaze fixed on the curved tarpaulin. His main suspect in the murder of Gina Gloger had just been fished out of the North Sea. Which raised several more questions than what Jesko had been doing out there.

"And it's quite certain that it's Jesko Mudder?" he inquired of Anja Wilkens, who apparently preferred to refrain from taking a closer look at the malodorous corpse on the spot.

"Yes. He still had his papers in his pocket."

"Which would not necessarily prove that it is really him," Büttner pointed out. "Maybe someone just wanted us to believe that it was him."

"Whatever. That's your job to find out." Anja Wilkens took her suitcase. "I'll take a closer look once it's on my desk." She wrinkled her nose. "I just wish you could disinfect him first, or at least give him a bubble bath."

"Eyes open when choosing a profession," Hasenkrug teased her. He too had dared a glance under the tarpaulin, but had just as quickly lowered it again. "Whew!" He turned towards the wind and took a deep breath of the fresh air. "Very well. I'll have a listen around then." When Hasenkrug saw the forensics crew coming, he pointed to the cutter directly in front of them. "Was it this cutter that made the … uh… catch?"

"Yep," both fishermen growled in unison.

"Whose is it?"

"Fokko Harms."

Hasenkrug frowned. "Is he related to Eiko Harms?"

"Jo."

"Jo."

"Aha. I didn't want to know that exactly. What is his relationship to Eiko Harms?"

"It's his father."

That might or might not be a coincidence, Büttner thought. "Was he washed into the net far out or rather near the coast?"

The two fishermen looked at each other, then shrugged. "No," one of them said, "far enough out, anyway, that swimming back would probably have been difficult." He looked at his mate. "Or what do you think, Hinnerk?"

"Jo."

"But Fokko, he can tell you more precisely. He also took

photos. So that everything is documented. After all, he said, "You don't want to be accused of anything afterwards."

"That means Mr Harms was also on board himself?"

"Jo."

"And where is he now?"

"On the cutter, I'd say. Or what do you think, Hinnerk?"

"Jo."

Büttner sighed. He would probably not be able to avoid taking a closer look at the scene of the incident anyway and having the captain explain to him how the whole thing had happened. But there was still time to do that when the forensic team had finished their work on the cutter, so tomorrow rather than today. Which was good because calmer weather was also forecast for tomorrow. Hopefully, the rocking of the cutter would not make him seasick right away, which could well have been the case today. It would be even better, he decided, to leave this part to Hasenkrug anyway.

Büttner didn't expect too much from securing the tracks, as any that might have existed had certainly long since been destroyed by the salty lake water and the rain, which barely paused. This is exactly what Chris Bäumler seemed to think, standing in front of the cutter with his men, frowning and shaking his head.

When an employee of the forensics department lifted the tarpaulin to photograph the corpse, he was not the only one to recoil with a curse and jump backwards. Everywhere, a horrified murmur went through the people standing on the quay. Some reflexively held their noses and tried to flee to a safe distance and, above all, in a direction away from the wind. This was also the case for Büttner and Hasenkrug.

"He definitely didn't spend much less time in the water than Gina Gloger," Hasenkrug moaned with a disgusted expression on his face when they had stowed their wet jackets in the boot shortly afterwards and were back in the car.

"I can't imagine that whoever disposed of him on the high seas assumed that he would ever resurface." Büttner reflected. He rubbed his nose and hoped that the unholy mixture of the smell of fish and decay had not settled into it forever. "He probably thought it was a safe bet to make him disappear that way."

"Karma is a bitch," said Hasenkrug. "And sometimes it even plays into our hands. If Jesko hadn't fallen into the fishermen's net, he would have been on the wanted list until doomsday."

"It's just too bad that he can't tell us now whether he killed Gina or not," Büttner growled. "It's also a pity that we can't hold him accountable for these unspeakable videos. That should be a pretty unsatisfactory situation for the women concerned."

"Unless they themselves helped in his demise," Hasenkrug qualified. "It is not impossible that at least one of them got wind of the matter and took revenge on him. We haven't spoken to most of these women yet. For example, with this riding therapist, Silvia Remmers."

"Which is why we're going back to the riding school now," Büttner said. He started the engine, switched on the windscreen wipers and ventilation and drove off when he could see through the windscreen again. "In the Jesko Mudder case we can't do much anyway, as long as we don't have the results of the forensic medicine. And then it's up to us to find out whether it's a double murder that we have to solve or whether Jesko might have had to die because he was responsible for Gina's death."

Hasenkrug wiped his face with a groan. "And these are only two of the possible variations that are conceivable. Unfortunately, it doesn't get any clearer than that."

"That's why I really hope Marieke finds out something in her undercover action," Büttner said. "If anyone can make the women from the riding school talk, it's her."

"A motive to kill Jesko Mudder also had Holger Moersler and, not to forget," Hasenkrug raise his index finger, "Eiko Harms. Somehow I don't want to believe that Jesko's body just happened to find itself in Eiko's father's fishing net."

Büttner frowned. "You think someone smuggled the body between the crabs? Hm. Quite apart from the fact that this is hardly conceivable in practice – why should the members of the Harms family, of all people, have an interest in the corpse returning home from the bosom of Neptune, when shortly before they were intent on digging him a sailor's grave in the North Sea?"

"This could all be a clever deception."

"Probably a confusing one rather than a clever one."

When they stopped again at the police cordon, the now dripping wet young colleague was still standing in place and did not look happy about it.

Büttner stopped and lowered the window, which did not make the man any happier when he recognised him. "Why are you still standing around here?" he wanted to know.

Briefly, the colleague seemed to consider whether it could be a trick question. "W-because no one has told me yet that the mission is over?" He stammered his answer with an audible question mark.

"Interesting. Did it ever occur to you that you might have been forgotten here?"

"Uh…"

"I see. If, contrary to expectations, you're not in bed with a feverish pneumonia tomorrow, why don't you ask your training officer when the lesson 'independent thinking' is on the syllabus for?" With that, Büttner raised the window again and accelerated.

16

As soon as they got out of the car at the riding school, Kira Grensemann came running up to them. "Is it true that Jesko was fished out of the North Sea?"

Büttner sighed inwardly. Just a moment ago he had considered whether it would not be better not to make Jesko Mudder's finding public for the time being, but he could probably forget that now. The bush drums in the Krummhörn apparently worked as reliably as ever. So it was pointless to deny it. "Who did you hear about it from?" He pulled the collar of his jacket tighter around him as a cold gust of wind swept across the yard. But at least it wasn't raining at the moment, so it couldn't hurt to be out in the fresh air for a bit, especially as he couldn't help feeling that the smell of the corpse was doing its business in his mucous membranes.

"Amke, Gina's mother, called me. She sounded really relieved.

"Relieved?"

"Yes, it's a pity that Jesko doesn't have to serve his sentence now," she shrugged, "but it's not a bad solution. At least he can't cause any more mischief now." She looked from one to the other, frowning. "What are you still doing here? Your case is closed, isn't it?"

"Well, when our case is closed is still for us to decide," Büttner countered her. "You seem to overlook the fact that we are now dealing with a second murder case."

The stud boss didn't seem to have thought that far ahead, because she looked at him in irritation. "And what if he had thrown himself into the North Sea?"

"Why would he have done that?"

"Because he didn't want to face his responsibilities, probably."

Büttner had no intention of getting involved in such a speculative discussion. However, he found her reaction quite revealing, as she obviously had some interest in the investigation not being taken further. "We would like to talk to … er… your riding therapist."

"Which one? There's more than one therapist going in and out of here." Her tone had cooled noticeably.

"Silvia Remmers," said Hasenkrug when he noticed that his boss once again did not have the name ready.

"That won't work," Kira Grensemann waved it off. "She's in a therapy session right now."

"Well, we can wait," Büttner said. "A good opportunity to talk to your riding students again."

"Because of those unspeakable videos?"

Büttner tried not to let his surprise show. Did they talk about everything and everyone here? At least as far as the pornographic videos were concerned, he would have assumed that the young women preferred to keep this information to themselves in order to digest it first. He pointed to the pit stall. "Are they there?"

"Who exactly are you referring to?"

"Uh…"

"Tomke, Sanna and Lisa," Hasenkrug helped out again.

"They've gone again. I don't think they'll be back today either."

Hasenkrug nodded absently and furrowed his brow. Büttner followed his gaze. A woman in riding clothes stepped out of the box stall who looked familiar to Büttner, but he was not immediately able to classify her. Only when she looked him straight in the eye and then stopped walking did he know where to place her. It was Gina's mother's friend.

"Wiebke Storm rides here too?" asked Hasenkrug.

"Yes, for many years. Just like Tomke. Why?"

"What does Mrs Storm have to do with Tomke?" Hasenkrug inquired.

"She's her mother."

"Is that so?"

Büttner briefly wondered why this information had not yet been passed on to them by their colleagues, even though they had the task of investigating the riders. But then he remembered that Tomke was the only one of Gina's friends who did not appear in one of the porn videos, so she was not at the top of the list of suspects.

"Hello, Mrs Storm," he called to the woman, without knowing what exactly he wanted from her. But somehow his gut feeling told him that it would be important to take a closer look at her.

"Hello," she greeted them, but seemed undecided whether she should join them or leave. Judging by her expression, she was not happy to find them here.

"We have a few questions for you," Büttner did not let her off the hook. "If you could spare us a few minutes…"

"I'm afraid I'm in a hurry!"

"All right, then tomorrow morning at eight at the police station."

She came towards them, albeit hesitantly.

"How are the Glogers?", Büttner asked an innocuous question when she was directly opposite him.

"How are parents supposed to feel who have just lost their child."

Büttner waited for her to say more, but she remained silent. "I meant more about how they took the news that Jesko Mudder had been found dead."

"I don't know, I haven't spoken to them since." She pointed her riding crop over to a bright red VW. "I just found out about it and was about to head over to them now."

Büttner saw no reason to detain her any longer, even though his stomach continued to sound the alarm in her presence. But he still had too little information about her to be able to ask purposeful questions. Therefore, he only nodded and said, "Do that. The Glogers can use all the support they can get."

As Wiebke Storm sped away in her car shortly afterwards, Kira Grensemann glanced at her wristwatch, not exactly furtively, and said, "Well, I'd better be off, there's a lot to do." She raised a brow, which gave her, no doubt not entirely unintentionally, a certain arrogance. "I think you can manage on your own?"

"Yes, thank you, we are big enough," Büttner couldn't help saying.

Kira Grensemann threw her head back and stalked off without a greeting. As friendly and approachable as she had been when they first met, right now she reminded Büttner of her arrogant son Christopher – who, as they had found out in the meantime, had not only once had a run-in with the law.

On the way here, Hasenkrug had received the news from his colleagues that Christopher Grensemann had already violated the narcotics law several times and was also no stranger to the vice squad's area of responsibility. Apparently, he liked to spend his weekends in Hamburg, where he not only gained a lot of experience with drugs and women, but also with gambling. The latter with little success, which had brought him considerable trouble here and there, up to and including a stay in hospital after a brawl. Therefore, Büttner thought it likely that Christopher had known about Jesko's internet activities. He had possibly even earned money from it, in whatever form. However, he did not appear on the porn site's client list, which the colleagues had already checked. Unfortunately, the evidence for a house search at the Grensemanns' was still not sufficient.

"Well, let's see how the riding therapist will react to the porn video," Büttner said. He preceded Hasenkrug into the riding stable. His first glance caught Silvia Remmers, who was leading a horse on a lunge. A smile crept onto his face when he noticed that it was Marieke, who was doing her therapy lesson. The two were talking animatedly and apparently getting along well, because now they were both laughing happily.

When their eyes met immediately afterwards, Büttner nodded to his colleague, whereupon she greeted cautiously. She drew Silvia Remmers' attention to her. She also greeted him, but then immediately concentrated on her work again.

Büttner let his gaze wander through the riding hall. Lessons were taking place in the neighbouring riding arena. Four girls of primary school age were practising vaulting there, some of which looked adventurous. One of them seemed to be completely fearless, because she even dared to do a headstand on the horse's back. Of course, she was secured and supported by an adult woman whom Büttner did not know; but he was still impressed by the little girl's courage.

"Take a look up to the rider's room without attracting attention," Hasenkrug asked his boss, without looking in the indicated direction.

Büttner let a few seconds pass, then he lifted his gaze. "Hm," he then observed, "that looks like anything but a harmonious partnership. And besides, didn't Mrs Grensemann claim that Sanna was no longer here?"

Behind the glass sliding elements of the riding room, Sanna and Christopher stood in front of each other and seemed to be involved in a heated argument. It even went so far that Sanna shoved both hands against her boyfriend's chest, causing him to stagger dangerously. But at least he refrained from paying her back in similar coin, only shouting at her with gestures. Unfortunately, not a single sound reached them downstairs, so it was impossible to say whether this argument had anything to do with the news of Jesko's death, which had spread like wildfire.

So Büttner concentrated on Marieke again. Just as he was wondering how long her therapy session would last, Silvia Remmers left them alone and ran off towards the common room. Marieke waited until she had disappeared around the corner, then she waved her colleagues over.

Büttner and Hasenkrug quickly approached her and the horse.

"Just for a moment," Marieke hissed at them. "Silvia will be right back, she's getting my water bottle. If you're here to talk to her, you'd better leave. I've arranged to meet her for a coffee under the pretext of having to discuss something about the therapy. We'll sit together in the riding room right after this lesson."

Involuntarily, Büttner's gaze wandered upwards again, but Sanna and Christopher had disappeared.

"I think I can learn some things from her that will help us. She trusts me."

"Does she know about the video yet?" asked Hasenkrug.

"Yes. She's … well … quite shocked."

"But who told her about it?" wondered Büttner. "After all, we only gave the other women their own …"

"I don't think Holger will come here again this week," Marieke interrupted him in a raised voice. "Why don't you try him at home?"

Irritated for a moment, Büttner now saw that Silvia Remmers was coming back. So that's why Marieke's diversionary manoeuvre. She was really on her toes.

Silvia Remmers eyed her suspiciously. "Would you like to join me?"

"No," Hasenkrug said without hesitation, and Büttner

nodded. "Rather, we are looking for Holger Moersler. But we've already been told that he probably won't be coming here this week."

"What do you want from Holger?" The therapist suddenly looked nervous.

"He'll find out from us," Büttner replied. "And now we won't disturb you any longer." He nodded to Marieke. "All the best to you.

"Thank you."

"Silvia Remmers is probably a few years older than Jesko's other lovers," Hasenkrug noted as they stepped out of the riding hall. "Oh, shit, can't it even be good with the rain!" he cursed and fumbled for his hood. Sure enough, the dark clouds were just pouring a torrential downpour on them. So they hurried to get into their vehicle.

"Yes, she must be in her mid-thirties, if not forties," Büttner elaborated on his assistant's observation as soon as they were in the car. The rain pelted the bodywork so loudly that he had to raise his voice. "What do the colleagues say? Haven't they checked her out yet?"

Hasenkrug looked at his smartphone. After some swiping and typing, he said, "She's thirty-eight, so fifteen years older than Jesko."

"And here's to you, Mrs Robinson," Büttner quietly sang the first line of the title song of the well-known Hollywood film from the sixties.

"Nice allusion," said Hasenkrug, amused. "But the age difference between Benjamin Braddock and Mrs Robinson must have been many a year greater."

"Still, one wonders what motivated the therapist to engage in a sexual relationship with the much younger Jesko Mudder."

Hasenkrug pocketed his smartphone again. "Jesko was an attractive man. So why shouldn't she get involved with him? I really wonder why such a relationship in reverse – that is, when the man is so much older – would hardly have inspired a remark, but in a mixed situation like this it immediately seems suspect. Maybe they just fancied each other."

"And Mudder also had ulterior motives," Büttner said. "I could imagine that he wanted to expand the target group for his videos through her."

"Possible. In any case, it is interesting that Silvia Remmers already knows about the video. So someone else besides us must know that this film exists. Christopher Grensemann, perhaps?"

"Maybe. Let's wait and see what Marieke finds out. Maybe Silvia Remmers will mention who let her share his knowledge."

"And now?" asked Hasenkrug.

"Now it's closing time," Büttner replied. "Jette wants to tell us about Cape Town via Zoom. And I don't intend to miss that."

17

David Büttner looked at his wife in disappointment. He had hurried to be home on time, and now this. "Two hours later? But why is that?" He looked at his watch. It was just after six, they had been supposed to meet Jette at half past six. Now it would be half past eight.

"It's a beautifully warm and sunny day in Cape Town," Susanne explained. She poured him a coffee and placed it in front of him on the kitchen table. "Jette and Debbie still want to go to the beach together as soon as Debbie has finished her last lesson."

"Hm." Büttner wondered why it had to be today of all days, when his daughter was planning to spend several months there. The beach wasn't going to run away from her! "But the water at the Cape is surely still much too cold. After all, it was still winter there."

"Jette will know what she is doing. She might not even want to go into the water, but just sit on the beach. And if she goes in the water, she'll notice pretty quickly whether it's warm enough or not."

Büttner couldn't stand it when his wife had an answer for everything and brought up arguments that he found hard to resist.

"I'm so glad that Jette has settled in so well already and

gets on so well with Debbie." Susanne smiled with satisfaction. "Aren't you too, David?"

"Hmm."

"Now don't look so unhappy." She raised two fingers. "It's only two hours, David. So no need to go all drama queen on me. Do you think bacon pancakes for dinner might cheer you up?" she added without transition.

Since bacon pancakes could cheer him up at any time of the day or night, he nodded delightedly.

"Good." Immediately she took some eggs from the fridge. "Would you mind taking Heinrich out while I'm busy here? He hasn't had much of a run today."

The dog had heard his name. He raised his head and pricked up his ears. He looked expectantly from one to the other.

Büttner glanced out of the window. It had been dark for a long time, but the moon, still almost full, gave a pale light. In the cone of light from the streetlamp, he saw that the rain seemed to be taking a break. He quickly took a few more sips of coffee, then stood up and came back immediately with the leash and torch in his hand. "Come on, Heinrich," he said to the delight of his dog, who now, seized with sudden eagerness, jumped out of the basket and ran towards him wagging his tail. "We'll go for another round of the meadows. A bit of fresh air will do us both good."

He walked Heinrich along the road, then turned into a path that would lead him directly to the cattle pastures adjacent to the settlement. There he could easily let Heinrich off the leash at this time of year, and the dog would romp himself tired. He wouldn't get too far away from him anyway, so he wouldn't lose sight of him despite the darkness. No matter how old Heinrich was, he probably wouldn't let himself be deprived of his romp until his last day. He loved it far too much to jump freely through life and sniff out everything that came under his nose.

When the dog stopped at a rather squashed-looking molehill and began to dig with his front paws, Büttner also paused and, with his eyes closed, sucked the fresh, salty air that was drifting across the flat land from the sea deep into his lungs. You could think what you wanted about East Frisia – especially at this time of year – but it was certain that the air smelled as good as it did here in only a few places in Germany.

When he opened his eyes again, he was almost scared to death, because in front of him, as if from nowhere, stood a person with a corpulent stature. Since there was not much light coming from the settlement and he had switched off his torch, he could not make out much more than their contours. So he switched the torch back on, briefly illuminating the figure – which was clearly a woman – but then kept it pointed at the ground. "Can I help?"

"Please excuse me, Commissioner," said the woman, "I didn't mean to frighten you. I just didn't know how …" She stood with her head down and shrugged lamely. As the moon now disappeared behind the clouds, she switched on her headlamp, whereupon Büttner positioned himself so that it did not blind him. "Well, what can I say." She raised her head, tears shimmering in her eyes. "You are Commissioner Büttner, aren't you?"

"Um…" Büttner could not remember ever having seen

this woman anywhere before. Which, given his spotty memory, didn't mean too much, but still … He squinted at Heinrich. But he was still busy clearing away the molehill. Apparently the dog did not consider the situation threatening. "Good morning, Mrs… uh…"

"Mudder. Antje Mudder."

"Mudder." Büttner tilted his head. Was it possible that …?

"I am Jesko's mother," she confirmed his hunch. "My boy was … they took him … they took him … today." She put her hands to her face and burst into tears.

"Uh… my condolences." This encounter came as such a surprise that Büttner could think of nothing else to say.

"Thank you. I can't believe it yet. I know my Jesko was no saint," she whimpered through her fingers. "Ever since I can remember, there's been trouble with him. It started in kindergarten and never stopped." She lifted her tear-veiled gaze. "But he was still my child. And no one has the right to take my child away from me like that. No one!"

"I understand that," Büttner replied. "But how …" He circled the night-black landscape with his arms. "I mean … uh … did you follow me?"

She nodded.

"So you were waiting for me outside my house?"

"I … I know that this is not the right thing to do. You just don't do that. I would never do it otherwise."

"But?"

"I didn't want to come to you at the police station." She looked around furtively, as if she feared that someone might overhear her. But far and wide there was not a soul to be seen. That might have been because the rain had started again.

"What's wrong with our police station?" inquired Büttner when she didn't continue speaking but just stood there with her shoulders drooping and shaken by sobs.

"The people. Ever since they found that girl … Gina's her name, I guess. Anyway … since they found her dead in the Greetsiel harbour basin, people have been pointing their fingers at me. In my neighbourhood, while shopping, everywhere. It's as if everyone suddenly knows me. Some of them shout at me that I should be ashamed of having such a son. They call Jesko a fucking murderer. I don't dare leave the house anymore. I didn't want to go somewhere where people were already pointing their fingers at me again."

"And that's why you ambush me in private? And what would you have done if I hadn't gone outside with my dog?"

"Then I would have rung your bell."

Her words were dramatic, as if it were a matter of life and death for her. Büttner, however, in no way thought that her reasoning justified visiting him in his private home after work.

Heinrich had razed the molehill to the ground. He lost interest and walked further along the dirt road, his nose always on the ground. Büttner also started moving again, the woman joined him without being asked.

"It's about my boy," she said so quietly that it was barely audible against the rustling of the wind and the splashing of the rain. "I … I just want things to be fair."

"And what do you think would be fair?"

"That my boy is not wrongly accused. Jesko came to see

me. He said that he found Gina dead in his bathtub when he came home, but that he had had nothing to do with her death. He was all nervous."

Büttner stared at her, perplexed. "Jesko came to you and told you that Gina was dead in his bathtub?"

She nodded.

"When was that?"

She looked at him as if he was dumbfounded. "Well, when Gina was dead in the bathtub."

Büttner took a deep breath and closed his eyes for a brief moment. "I meant on what day and at what time Jesko came to see you."

"I see." She wrinkled her nose, then said, "That was Monday. It was quite late. Around midnight, I'd say."

"And you didn't find it necessary to call the police?" Büttner didn't want to believe it.

"No. Jesko told me not to do anything until he told me to. And that he'd do it then, that he'd call the police when he was far enough away."

Well, Jesko definitely hadn't done that. Either because he didn't really intend to, or because he couldn't anymore, since he himself had long been dead. They would probably find out tomorrow from the forensics department what the situation was.

Büttner shook his head in bewilderment. If the emergency services had found Gina in the bathtub on Monday night, no one would have had time to get her body into the Greetsiel harbour basin. It might even have been possible to catch her murderer trying to get the body out of the house. "It must be clear to you that you have massively hindered the investigation with this delay. There will be consequences, Mrs Mudder."

"But I only did it for Jesko." She looked at him pleadingly. "A mother can't betray her child, that's not possible. After all, someone has to stand by the boy."

Büttner cursed inwardly. Could such behaviour be explained by motherly love, or was it simply abysmal stupidity? In any case, this woman did not seem to be the brightest candle on the cake. "But this is not a stupid boy's prank, it's murder, Mrs Mudder!" he said with a good portion of sharpness in his voice.

She nodded silently, but there was nothing to suggest that she was actually aware of the part she played in the mess.

"Did Jesko then suggest who might be responsible for Gina's death if it wasn't himself?"

"No. He wouldn't tell me."

"That means he knew?"

"I don't know if he knew. He certainly didn't say so." She clasped her fingers together as if she had to hold on to them. "Jesko told me not to tell anyone or do anything because then they'd definitely suspect him. Because Gina and he were a couple. He was so afraid that they would want to kill him too."

Büttner listened up. "That who wants to kill him? Did he mention names?"

"No. He just said he had to get away. That otherwise they'd kill him too. Or that you," she pointed her finger at Büttner, "that you'd put him in prison for something he didn't even do. He asked if I could give him money so he could go into hiding for a while."

"Well, did you?"

"What?"

"Gave him money."

"Of course I did. He is my boy after all. How else could it have worked? Jesko never had anything to spare, did he?" She dug out a crumpled handkerchief and blew her nose.

"When did you learn that Gina's body had been recovered from the dock?"

"My neighbour came over and told me. She's an old gossip, and at first I didn't believe her and rather looked on the Internet to see if there was anything there. Unfortunately, this time she was right. I wonder how Gina got there, when she was still in the bathtub before." She looked at him as if he should know the answer. Didn't she realise that she was talking her head off?

Next, Antje Mudder abruptly threw her head back and sobbed in despair. "And now … now my boy …" She did not finish the sentence, but instead brought her hand to her mouth and bit the back of her hand, as if she could numb the mental pain that raged inside her.

Büttner was convinced that Jesko had simply exploited his mother's good faith so that she would give him money and he could make off without hindrance. That would suit his character more than the alleged concern for her. "And where did Jesko want to go?"

"He didn't tell me that, of course. He told me it was better not to know in case someone asked me about it. He wanted to protect me."

"Indeed."

"Yes." She nodded emphatically. "Jesko wasn't a bad boy. A little wild sometimes, maybe, but not a bad boy."

Büttner briefly considered telling her about the videos that her son had made available to some horny men without the knowledge of his sex partners, but then decided against it. As blind as the woman seemed to be towards her son, there was no reason at this point to plunge her into an even deeper emotional hole. His task was merely to concentrate on her statement and draw his conclusions from it. For that, it was not necessary to make her fall over the cliff she was clinging to so desperately in her grief.

"So Jesko told you that someone was threatening him with death?", Büttner made sure. If that was the case, then Gina's murder and Jesko's murder might have been motivated by the same thing.

"Yes, that's what I'm saying. But I don't know from whom. He didn't give a name. I would tell you if I knew. Or do you think I could find his …" She swallowed hard, "I would just let his murderer get away with it?"

Büttner did not answer. Instead, he whistled for Heinrich, who immediately came running. The dog was no longer scurrying back and forth so excitedly. On the one hand, because he was probably tired; on the other, because he didn't like rain very much either. So it was a good time to head back before the bacon pancakes got cold or he might miss the chat with Jette.

"I just wanted you to know that," Antje Mudder let herself be heard after a long silence. "That you know my son is not a murderer."

That he *claimed* not to be a murderer, Büttner corrected this statement in his mind, but he did not say it out loud. He didn't quite believe Jesko's version of the story yet. Or was it even his mother's version? "Did you know Gina personally?" he asked.

She shook her head. "No. It hadn't been going on that long with the two of them. And at some point, I stopped asking him about his girlfriends. He was always coming on to me with someone else." She laughed mirthlessly. "My Jesko had a way with women, that's for sure."

A bit much of a way for Büttner's taste, but that didn't belong here either. "Did Jesko tell you that Gina was pregnant?" By now it was clear that Jesko had indeed been the father of the child.

To his surprise, the woman nodded. "Yes. And that upset him even more."

"That she was pregnant?"

"No. That now the child is dead too. He said to me that he was looking forward to becoming a father. That he would then finally have a job that he enjoyed."

Büttner was not sure whether he should believe that. For all he knew about Jesko, it didn't seem to be in his nature to take responsibility for other people. But perhaps even he had had a soft side.

Having arrived at the settlement, Büttner said goodbye to Antje Mudder.

"Thank you for listening to me," she whispered with her head bowed. "And sorry again for bothering you at closing time. But I really didn't mean to …" She raised her shoulders and dropped them again in resignation.

"It's all right, Mrs Mudder," he said conciliatorily. "I thank you for telling me all that. It certainly helps us."

She looked at him with hope. "You will find my boy's killer, won't you?"

"You can be sure that we are doing everything in our power," he replied evasively.

She nodded and walked across the street to her small car, which was parked exactly opposite Büttner's house.

"You look so thoughtful," Susanne noted when Büttner came into the kitchen a little later, where it smelled deliciously of fresh bacon pancakes. Heinrich jumped straight into his basket, curled up and closed his eyes in exhaustion. Trude the cat joined him and began to lick his fur dry.

Büttner put two plates on the table and added cutlery. Then he sat down and told his wife in a few sentences what had happened on his walk.

"Things happen!" Susanne said, shaking her head. "So now two mothers have already lost their child. How awful!" She scooped a pancake onto his plate.

Yes, it was terrible. But also opaque, as Büttner found. That evening, however, he didn't want to think about it any longer, because after all, tomorrow was another day. So, he grabbed a knife and fork and began to eat with a big appetite.

Jette looked good-humoured and fresh, and she was beaming all over. Büttner's scepticism had still not necessarily given way to euphoria about his daughter being on the other side of the world, yet he immediately felt more conciliatory in view of her obvious cheerfulness.

"Is it really as beautiful as you imagined?" he inquired, although the question was actually unnecessary given the gleam in her eyes.

"Oh, Pops," Jette enthused, "I wish you could see all this. It's just perfect here and even more beautiful than I had imagined. Great people, bright sunshine, sparkling sea, fantastic scenery, pure life … you can't get much more. And Debbie is just a darling." She looked to the side and waved someone over.

Immediately afterwards, a petite person with light, shoulder-length hair and tanned skin slid into view. Debbie waved briefly, and with her warm smile she managed to win Büttner over from one moment to the next. "Hello, nice to meet you. How are you?"

While Büttner was still rummaging through his brain for a suitable answer and had to realise that his knowledge of English was even more marginal than he had always imagined, Susanne answered Debbie's question by return and immediately followed it up with a few more sentences. The three women promptly found themselves in a conversation that, although not entirely fluent on Susanne's and Jette's part, was still somewhat comprehensible.

Büttner quickly realised that he could not keep up with the pace at which the women were talking to each other. As soon as he had put together his English sentence, the three of them had long since moved on to another topic. Still, it would have been extremely rude to Debbie to just continue chatting in German. So he decided to just sit there as an onlooker and listen to what Jette had to say about her first day in Cape Town, because his English was good enough to listen and understand.

There was a lot of joking and laughing, and as soon as Jette or Susanne had a hitch, with Debbie's help they quickly figured out the right wording for what they wanted to express. She seemed to be a careful teacher. More prudent, Büttner thought, than the English teachers he had had to endure in his long past school career. He wondered, not for the first time, why students at Germany's state schools were often bothered with teachers who clearly didn't know their job, but then handed out grades that were supposed to tell the students they were too stupid to learn.

Before Büttner knew it, an hour had passed. When he closed his laptop, he felt much more relaxed than before the conversation.

Susanne pressed a kiss to his cheek. "You see, David, our child is fine. Calmed down?"

Büttner nodded. Yes, he felt much better after the bacon pancakes and the chat, which was as entertaining as it was relaxed. He stood up and uncorked a bottle of red wine. Immediately afterwards, he handed Susanne a glassful and toasted her. "Thank you for putting up with me despite everything."

18

When David Büttner came into the office the next morning, not only Sebastian Hasenkrug but also Marieke de Boer was already there. Marieke was sitting in a wheelchair, which, Büttner noted regretfully, certainly indicated that she was having one of her worse days. "Everything okay so far?" he asked. "I'm amazed that you're up so early … er…" He faltered as he realised his faux pas. "Sorry."

Marieke laughed. "No problem, boss." She grabbed the tyres of her wheelchair with her hands. "Every now and then I should give my body a break, my physiotherapist says. So sometimes I'm out with my crutches – which is really tiring – and sometimes I'm out with this contraption." She dug a USB stick out of her pocket and held it up. "It's got some info on it summarised that I've been researching about the ladies at the equestrian centre." She held it out to Hasenkrug, who stood up and took it from her. "But actually I'm here to tell you what I learned from Silvia Remmers."

"But you're still on sick leave, Marieke," Büttner admonished her, "so you shouldn't be here at all."

"I just came by for a little chat," Marieke replied with a shrug. "No one can object to that. It's good for the convalescence." She sipped her coffee and then nodded appreciatively. "Wow, the new machine is really better than the old one. It tastes totally good." She set the cup aside and patted her thighs. "So …"

Büttner raised his hand. "Before you start, I would like to inform you both about something that happened to me last night, or rather who happened to me last night."

"Happened?" Hasenkrug raised his brows. "That doesn't sound good."

"As you can see, I survived. No, joking aside. When I was out with Heinrich, Jesko Mudder's mother ambushed me."

Now he had the full attention of his colleagues. So he reported in short sentences what he had learned from Antje Mudder.

"Wow," Hasenkrug said when Büttner had finished. "So if we assume it happened the same way, we're looking for a double murderer. Which would also mean that Jesko is out as Gina's killer and probably didn't commit suicide either."

Büttner raised his index finger. "*If* we assume that her story is true, yes. But it could just as well be that Jesko killed his girlfriend and then told his mother some story to get money out of her and get away. Or that she invented this story to clear her son, although she knows very well that he is Gina's murderer. It's just a statement, that's all."

"But she knew about the bathtub," Marieke pointed out. "That's factual insider knowledge, isn't it?"

"Right." Büttner nodded. He hadn't thought that far ahead. Cape Town had probably distracted him too much. "In fact, nothing of this should be known to the public yet. If Antje Mudder knows that Gina didn't drown in the harbour basin but in the bathtub …"

"… then Jesko must also have known," Hasenkrug finished the sentence. "That means he either killed Gina himself, or the story he told his mother is true."

"The latter would be supported by the fact that he himself is now dead," Marieke said. "Unless there is someone who promptly avenged Gina's death. Eiko Harms and Holger Moersler, for example, would have a motive for that."

"The autopsy report is coming in here right now," Hasenkrug announced. "Maybe it will give us a clue as to how much longer Jesko lived than Gina." He played the file on the big screen.

They took their time to skim the report first.

"He did not drown, but was hit with a blunt object," Büttner finally broke the silence. "It is also not impossible that he fell and hit his head. In any case, the result was a fracture of the base of the skull, which ultimately led to death if left untreated. From this we can then probably conclude that someone wanted his body to disappear into the North Sea. A suicide is therefore ruled out."

Hasenkrug grimaced. "It would have been better if he had not done the sinking in the fishing grounds of the crab fishermen."

"Anja puts the time of death between one and three o'clock in the night from Tuesday to Wednesday," Büttner brought up the next fact. "So Jesko died about one day after Gina. Quite obviously, on the night his mother claims he was with her, he didn't manage to make off somewhere where the killer wouldn't find him. All in all, Antje Mudder might actually have been right with her story."

"All we need now is the motive for the murders," Marieke said. "Not to mention the murderer or murderers."

Büttner leaned back in his chair. "Yes. Now we know a bit more, but we're still not much smarter." He looked at Marieke. "You spoke to the riding therapist? Did she have anything interesting to contribute?"

Marieke swayed her head back and forth. "I don't know if what I know now is really interesting for our case. After all, Silvia and I just chatted a bit. If I had made an interrogation out of it, she would have become suspicious. But of course I still tried to find out something without her getting suspicious. And I think I succeeded. However, Silvia likes to gossip about others, which was quite helpful in this case. She certainly seems to have quite a bit of anger in her belly."

Büttner looked at her expectantly. To his knowledge, it had never happened that Marieke had not decisively advanced one of her cases, no matter how she had obtained the information. These ways had been manifold – and certainly not always legal. But if it served to find the truth …

Büttner had long since ceased to see his young colleague's unconventional approach as reprehensible as he should. Over time, he had become more relaxed about this. The fact was that many a murderer would certainly still be walking around free today if he, as Marieke's boss, hadn't turned a blind eye – or both – every now and then and instead stuck to the letter of the law. "So?" he asked her to speak.

"As I said before, Silvia knows about the porn videos."

"So you called her on it again?"

"Nah, I didn't have to. She herself started talking about it again. I think she had to leave her pent-up anger somewhere." Marieke laughed out. "And angry she was, that's for sure. *If Jesko wasn't already dead anyway, I would have let him vent sooner or later.* Those were her exact words."

"When exactly did she find out about the videos?"

"She knew about it before Gina died." Marieke paused briefly to jerk herself into a different sitting position. "So here's where it gets interesting, guys," she then said. "It was Christopher Grensemann who tipped her off. And it was exactly four days ago, so not too long before Gina and Jesko died."

"So Grensemann actually knew about the videos." Büttner nodded. "That's what I thought. Which possibly indicates that not only Jesko, but also he made money from it economically. Silvia Remmers didn't happen to comment on that?"

"Grensemann allegedly told Silvia that he had just found out about the videos. He must have acted shocked and claimed that it was important to him that she found out about it."

"If he was so shaken," Büttner pondered, "why did he only tell Silvia and not the other women?"

"And above all, why didn't he press charges then?" asked Hasenkrug. "Or Silvia?"

"I asked Silvia the same thing."

"Well?"

"She says Christopher and she had another plan to get back at Jesko," Marieke explained. "What that plan was, she wouldn't reveal."

"Blackmail," Büttner said promptly. "What else could it be? You and Grensemann wanted to uncover their knowledge. But now a dead Jesko Mudder is of no use to them. After all, corpses are generally difficult to blackmail."

"Maybe that's why Silvia is so angry with Jesko," Hasenkrug mused. "By killing him, he screwed up a lucrative business deal for her."

"How unfair of him," Büttner grinned.

"Whatever," Marieke said. "The fact is that Silvia knew about the videos. And maybe she just made up this alleged other plan to distract from the suspicion that she might have had something to do with Jesko's murder because of the video."

"Yes, that would be possible. So we should definitely stay on it. I would say that another conversation with Grensemann is due in this regard. Is there anything else you learned from Silvia Remmers?"

"Well, if you ask me, boss, she had a huge crush on Jesko. The fact that he was just messing with her doesn't seem to have changed that."

"You just said she wanted to kill Jesko," Hasenkrug reminded her.

"Which is not mutually exclusive," Marieke replied. "Love and hate are known to be very close together. I would even say that the disappointment for Silvia, should she really love him, would be even greater than for the other women who were so badly treated by Jesko. Maybe she just went crazy when she found out about the videos and in her frustration killed not only Jesko but also Gina."

"Why Gina?"

Marieke shrugged her shoulders. "Jealousy? Always a popular motive."

"Would you trust her with the murders?" asked Büttner.

"If she is unscrupulous enough to blackmail someone, she has a certain criminal energy. So she can't be that harmless. Although a murder or even a double murder are of course a completely different matter. In any case, I wouldn't exclude her from the circle of suspects."

"Did you have a chance to check her alibi?"

"Nah, that didn't happen."

"Then we will definitely have to talk to her again, too." Büttner picked up the phone and asked Mrs Weniger to call Silvia Remmers for the next day. Although he wished that the case would be solved by then, he did not want to assume that for the time being. He could still cancel the summons.

"Good," said Hasenkrug, "then we still have Sanna, Tomke and Lisa. Were you able to find out anything about the three of them?"

Marieke grinned. "Sure. I already said that Silvia likes to talk. About others, too. And since she was really into it anyway because of Jesko, she naturally also worked off the women Jesko was chasing as well. Especially Sanna and Lisa, who can also be seen in the videos. Which must have surprised Silvia, because she says she didn't even realise that they had anything going on with Jesko.

"She is actually jealous of them, even though they are only victims too?" asked Büttner.

"She wished plague and cholera and much worse on Lisa and Sanna." Marieke frowned. "I was really surprised because she was suddenly so different from the therapist I had known her as. I really thought she was much gentler. But apparently that's mostly what she is to horses."

"Two souls dwell, alas, in my breast," Hasenkrug borrowed a quote from Goethe's Faust. "And what did she have to say about the other three women?

Marieke shrugged her shoulders. "Only the worst. She seemed intent on stomping the three of them into the ground in front of me. For example, she laughed herself half to death because Sanna and Lisa failed their exams."

"That really doesn't show good character," Büttner had to admit. "And what exactly did she find so funny about it?"

"She said they always acted so harmless. Supposedly they were always the teacher's favourites. But then they must have cheated in the final exams."

"And what is this alleged fraud supposed to have looked like?" inquired Büttner.

Marieke waved her hand. "No, no, boss, you can delete the 'allegedly' right away. I have researched this. It's been proven that Lisa and Sanna had the assignments, including the solutions, for the written A-levels exam for the maths advanced course before the exam. That's why they were disqualified."

"Huh?" Büttner looked at her incredulously. "How is that supposed to work? As far as I know, the assignments are at the ministry until the day of the exam and are only passed on to the schools immediately before the exam. That doesn't really leave any time to prepare."

"Yes, it is strange. There must have been someone who gave them the tasks. But the two of them didn't say anything about it, and even vehemently denied that they had nothing to do with the fraud. But I would have done the same in their place."

"And how did they come up with the scam? Did they get the highest score?"

"No. It didn't even get that far. There was an anonymous tip-off and that's how they got busted before they even wrote the exam."

"Extremely suspicious," Büttner said.

Hasenkrug screwed up his face. "I'm much more interested in what makes you tick to choose maths as an advanced course. That sounds like a character flaw per se. Well, I wouldn't have got through the exam without a cheat sheet, that's for sure."

"Quite apart from that," Büttner said, "such fraud does not make someone a murderer."

"It was not my intention to connect the maths exams with the murders," Hasenkrug countered. "That would be a bit far-fetched." He furrowed his brow. "Although when I think back to my maths teachers …"

"Whatever," Marieke interrupted his train of thought. "If one thing is certain, it's that neither Gina nor Jesko had anything to do with the maths A-levels. Gina had English and chemistry as an advanced course, and Jesko never attended a grammar school."

"But Gina had also only graduated from high school this summer," Büttner thought he remembered. "So the three of them also knew each other from school and not just from the riding school?"

Marieke nodded. "Yes, the three of them – or four, because Tomke was also one of them – went to the same grammar school and had known each other for several years. Even before they started riding."

"Gina passed her A-levels, though, if I'm informed correctly."

"Yes. And Tomke too. They didn't cheat. Or at least didn't get caught."

"A nice excursion into the abysses of the human soul," said Büttner, "but unfortunately nothing that helps us."

The door was opened briskly after a short knock, and Mark Humboldt entered. "Oh, Marieke," he exclaimed, his whole face beaming, "what a joy!" He walked up to her and gave her a hug. Then he kicked the wheelchair lightly and said, "I thought you didn't need that fucking thing anymore."

"Then stop thinking," growled Büttner.

"Believe me, David, you don't want that. And in a moment you'll see why." Humboldt turned to Hasenkrug. "I sent you a video file. Can you play it on your great monitor?"

"More porn?" asked Büttner, who feared bad things.

"Nah. Different bad."

It took only a few seconds for Hasenkrug to track down and start the file.

"What on earth is that?!" Büttner leaned forward. "Is that Jesko making a fool of himself?"

"The one who is made a fool of, I would rather say," Marieke said. "Someone must have filmed it after all. And it doesn't look like Jesko knows about it. Where did you get the video, Mark?"

"From the depths of the internet," Humboldt replied,

sipping his coffee with relish. "The things you find there if you dig long enough. But wait and see, it gets better."

Büttner had little desire to look any further, because what he had seen so far was quite enough for him. The image of a completely naked Jesko Mudder, obviously completely drunk or drugged, staggering down some staircase with an equally naked woman unknown to them in his arms, was not exactly the image he wanted to have stored in his memories.

"Attention, change of scene," Humboldt announced.

And indeed, the camera now panned around to reveal two broadly grinning faces, as well as two thumbs up.

"Sanna and Lisa," Marieke noted.

After this scene, the film was over.

"Perpetrator-victim reversal," Büttner noted. "When did this video appear on the net?"

"In December last year," Humboldt explained. "Uploaded from an anonymous account somewhere in Eastern Europe, so we can't trace where exactly it was launched. It spread like wildfire on social media, as you can imagine. The comments were appropriate, namely mostly gloating and way below the belt."

"Were any names mentioned?"

"Yes, Jesko Mudder's. First and last name along with links to all his social media accounts. Of course he did everything he could to delete it." Humboldt raised his arms. "But of course that doesn't work. Once on the net, always on the net."

"So Sanna and Lisa forwarded the recording and someone uploaded it. And probably on their behalf."

"You can certainly assume that," Humboldt said. "Only you would have to prove it to them. Maybe they've been hacked too, but that's unlikely."

"Did Jesko Mudder file a complaint?" Büttner could not remember seeing anything about this in his files.

"No, he apparently refrained from doing that. It would probably only have led to the video getting even more attention, and he wouldn't have wanted that. He had enough trouble as it was. Besides, he could never be sure that the story wouldn't backfire and his business with the videos would come to light."

"What kind of trouble has he been in?", Hasenkrug wanted to know.

"He lost his job."

"I thought he worked in a garage."

"This is his new job. He got it months later, after the dust had settled. But he was fired from his former workshop. His old boss found the unwanted attention a bit too much, which in the end not only Jesko but also his company received through the video."

"Do we know when the porn videos of the women appeared on the net?"

"Sanna's before and Lisa's shortly after this incident. So it's hardly likely that it was an act of revenge for that." Humboldt sighed. "I guess the two of them were just having some fun and the whole thing got out of hand."

"Well, we will ask her about it," said Büttner. "Jesko's popularity with the women doesn't seem to have been diminished, at least in the medium term. Amazing. Would really like to know what it was about the guy."

"Well," Marieke said, "at least someone must have been fed up with him, otherwise Jesko would hardly have ended up as by-catch in a fishing net."

Humboldt stood up. "Okay, everything else is your job. I have other things to do. Have fun with the puzzle."

Silence reigned in the room for quite a while. The whole story became more and more confusing. There were simply too many pieces on the board for Büttner's taste, and he had no idea whatsoever how to finish the game in a strategically clever way. Finally, he decided that a bit of fresh air would probably be quite good to clear his head.

"I'll be on my way to Greetsiel," he announced. "I'm going to get the captain of the fishing boat's teeth into it a bit, while you're trying to get some kind of order and preferably also logic into the information we now have."

Before he went out the door, he turned around again. "By the way, I didn't mean you, Marieke. You are on sick leave."

"You got it, boss." She winked at him mischievously. "I'm just here for a chat, after all."

19

The planks of the cutter were so slippery from the rain and spray that David Büttner would certainly have slipped on them more than once if he had not carefully felt his way forward, clinging to ropes, masts and whatever else promised support. He had to pay attention to every step, because there were numerous tripping hazards on board. The fact that the wind had picked up again and was driving dark, rain-heavy clouds across the sky didn't help either. It was a real dance on eggshells.

He had put on his rubber boots along with his knee-length mackintosh to be able to stand on the ship, but for some reason they failed him. They were probably made more for asphalt and concrete than for ship's planks. Or maybe the deck had only been moderately cleaned after the last sailing and that was why it was so slippery.

But Büttner preferred not to imagine that; if only because not long ago a corpse had lain on the planks, smelling pathetically of dead fish, and he imagined that he could smell its strong odour again. Of course, this could also have something to do with the fishing nets that fluttered in the wind and released extremely unpleasant odours.

"Will it be all right, Commissioner?" a man whom Büttner assumed to be the captain of the ship asked in a dark voice. Just as he had refused to come ashore at Büttner's request, he made no move to offer him help. Rather, he stood leaning against the cab with his arms folded, a hand-rolled cigarette stuck in the corner of his mouth. He was wearing his full fishing gear, but there was nothing to indicate that he would be leaving with his cutter any time soon. No one seemed to be on board except him, and even on the cutters around there was at best a leisurely bustle. There was no-one watching them, but nevertheless Büttner could not shake the feeling that a dozen pairs of eyes were directed at him.

"Fokko Harms?" he asked when he had finally made his way to the fisherman without an accident.

"Howdy," the man bellowed out instead of an answer.

"You are Fokko Harms, aren't you?", Büttner made sure, as he had no intention of talking to the false witness.

"Jo."

"It's about Jesko Mudder, who got into your net yesterday."

"Jo." Harms took a deep drag of his already quite well-burnt cigarette, then stubbed out the butt on a steel bar and threw it into a rusty tin can which, hanging on a string, rattled against one of the shrouds with every gust of wind. "Came as a surprise."

"Really?" Büttner eyed the man scrutinisingly. He was of beefy build, his round face weather-beaten, his eyes merely narrow slits above a broad, flat nose. He had something of a boxer about him. You could tell by looking at him that carrying an eighty-kilogram corpse from A to B shouldn't be too much trouble. Or hoisting it into a fishing net, if necessary.

"Yep. You don't really expect that kind of thing."

"How exactly do I have to imagine this?" asked Büttner.

"Huh? What now?"

"I meant, could you briefly explain to me how the whole thing went yesterday. You went out with your cutter, cast the nets on the high seas … and then?"

"Have we caught up with them again." Harms reached for a bright red thermos flask that stood next to him on a wooden trestle, unscrewed the lid and poured himself tea into it. Then he picked up a flat aluminium tin out of it, took a sandwich topped with ham and took a hearty bite.

Büttner waited for him to continue with the explanations, but he remained silent. "And after you had hauled the nets back in?" he huffed, forced to shout against the whistling of a fierce gust of wind as well as the pathetically crunching fenders and whirring shrouds.

The fisherman pointed amid ships to a large stainless steel container. "The nets are opened over there and the crabs fall in," he shouted back, now defying not only fenders and shrouds but also a screeching flock of seagulls. "Then the crabs run up the conveyor belt and is drummed for size."

The loud – and perhaps unusually wordy-talking seemed to have exhausted him, for he sighed audibly and first took a few sips of tea.

"And then?" Once again Büttner cursed the taciturnity of the East Frisians. Why could they never get their teeth apart? He could have been standing safely on the quay again long ago if the captain would just hurry up a bit when he spoke. But instead, because his ice-cold hands could no longer find a grip, he would probably be pushed across the deck and then over the railing by the next gust of wind, thus inevitably suffering the same fate as Gina Gloger. Man, man, man, what had possessed him to come here himself instead of sending Hasenkrug?!

"Well." Harms took a bite of his sausage sandwich and washed it down with his tea. "And then the crabs, that is, the one with the right size, goe back out through a tube and are cooked back there," he pointed to another container, "immediately. And when they're done cooking," he pointed to a hole in the stainless steel tub, "then they go into the refrigerator."

"Given the manageable size of the hole, I'm guessing Jesko Mudder didn't make it to the cold room."

Fokko Harms looked at him as if he had to check his state of mind. "Well", he then said. Suddenly, however, it seemed to dawn on him that Büttner might not have meant his remark entirely seriously, for he said with an amused twitch around his mouth, "Nah, he didn't even make it as far as cooking. Got dumped before that."

"And when exactly did Jesko get into your net?"

"Only on the last haul. Thank God, that's all I can say."

"Please?"

"Thank God for that."

"Yes, I had understood that."

The fisherman frowned and eyed him again with a good portion of scepticism.

"What is a haul?" asked Büttner impatiently.

"I see." Harms took off his cap and scratched the back of his head as if he had to think about the answer first, then he put his cap back on. "A haul is a catch."

"And you do several of these in a row, or how should I imagine?"

"Jo. One every hour."

"And so Jesko got into your net on the last haul."

"Yep. That's what I'm saying."

Büttner put his hand on the stainless steel tub. "And he ended up in here, too."

"Nah." Harms lit the next cigarette, which proved a little difficult in the stormy wind. "We saw right away that there were no crabs in the net this time. So at least there weren't much of them."

"Well?" Büttner's hands were numb with cold by now, but he didn't dare let go of the steel beam he was clinging to.

"Anyway. With Jesko inside, we preferred to open the net above deck, and he tumbled out." Harms did not give the impression that this rather untypical experience on the high seas had deprived him of sleep in the slightest. "Yep, and we all looked stupid."

Well, at least.

Harms made a dismissive gesture with his hand. "But we were just going back to the harbour anyway. We've been on the road long enough.

"When did you leave?"

"When did we cast off?"

Büttner hated quibbling over words. "Yes."

"Wednesday morning. Around four o'clock, I'd say."

"And where exactly did Jesko get into your net?"

"Borkum-Riffgrund. We were already on our way back, coming from Sylt."

"Hm. And when exactly did you make the last … er… haul?"

"Yesterday then, yes. Before we went back. Just before Borkum. It's not that far to Greetsiel then."

So the cutter had left at about the same time Jesko had been killed. Had his body possibly been transported with this cutter?

Büttner eyed the captain, but he was calm himself. There was nothing to suggest that the direction the conversation was taking made him nervous. On the other hand, what could make a real East Frisian nervous?

"Was your son also on board when you sailed?"

"Which son do you mean? I have three."

Crap! Of course, Büttner once again didn't have the right name. "I mean the one who was involved with Gina."

A shadow settled on Harms' face. "Nah. Eiko was on shift. With you. He doesn't travel with us much any more, de Fent." It was easy to hear that this did not suit the father. But perhaps he had done his son a favour by taking Jesko's body on board with him to send him over the planks on the high seas. But then why should he have brought it back with him?

"I could imagine that you didn't like the separation of Eiko and Gina," Büttner addressed the failed relationship of the two. "As Gina's parents told me, you had all assumed that the two would marry one day. You must have been pretty mad at Jesko for taking Gina away from your son."

"Hm." Harms didn't seem to want to answer. He drank tea.

"Would it also have had economic advantages for you and Gina's family if Eiko and Gina had married?"

Fokko Harms screwed his mug back onto the thermos. "Well, I have to go." Without so much as a glance at Büttner, he turned and stomped away with astonishingly sure steps over the rocking ship.

"So yes," Büttner answered himself. Then he did the egg dance back on land.

Since he had already been to Greetsiel, he took the opportunity to drive by the horse farm again. He wanted to talk to Christopher Grensemann and take this opportunity to find out Silvia Remmers' alibi – if he could find her. Which would be good, because then they could save themselves the interrogation the next day.

"Oh, the representative of the law again!" he heard a familiar, extremely snide-sounding voice behind him, accompanied by the slow clatter of hooves, as soon as he got out of the car. "Don't you ever give up?"

Büttner turned to Christopher Grensemann. The sweaty-looking young man wore mud-splattered riding clothes, held a crop in his hand and led a saddled horse on the reins, whose legs and underbelly were also completely filthy. He had obviously come back from a ride.

"It seems to bother you that we are trying to find the murderer of your friend Jesko. Will you tell me why?"

Grensemann seemed irritated for a brief moment, but quickly regained the usual arrogant expression on his face. "Who says that Jesko and I were friends? I really don't see what I should have to do with a woman-eating car mechanic."

Büttner wondered if this man knew any other language than this disrespectful one. Who did he actually think he was? And above all: how stupid did he think he was?

"Who are you trying to fool, Mr Grensemann? We know from various sources – one of which is your mother – that you had been friends with Jesko for many years, and very closely. It was even claimed that you two always knew everything about each other. That's why I have to wonder about your answer. May I ask if your amnesia has been bothering you for a long time, or is it a situational phenomenon?"

"Now don't be impertinent!" Grensemann harangued him. "Even if I had been such a close friend of Jesko's, as was allegedly claimed to you – what then was my motive to kill him?" He snorted contemptuously. "Don't make a fool of yourself!"

"Well, maybe you haven't been able to agree on who is entitled to the profits from the operation of the porn site," Büttner relied on the ruse tactic. It worked, because Grensemann's facial features slipped.

This time it took him longer to regain his composure, but he still tried to cover this moment of shock by laughing artificially. "You see me stunned, Commissioner. Did you say porn site? Sorry, but nothing is too stupid for you."

"Yes, it is. Porn sites, for example," Büttner didn't let himself get flustered, even if it cost him a great deal of effort in the face of this big shot. "Especially porn sites that the leading actresses don't even have a clue exist."

"I really have no idea what you have dreamed up." Grensemann was calm again. Which made little impression on Büttner, because his first reaction could hardly be misinterpreted.

"You might be interested to know that your friend Sanna

already knows about this site too. And I can assure you that she was not particularly thrilled to see herself there. But I assume she told you about it?"

"Once again, Commissioner," it came back much sharper after another few seconds of irritation, "I have no idea what you're making up. At any rate, I don't know what all this talk about a porn site is about." Grensemann held his index finger threateningly in front of his face. "And leave Sanna out of it. Turning her against me is the lowest form of behaviour!"

"At best, the lowest rail is what you have raised together with Jesko Mudder, Mr Grensemann."

"You can't do anything to me."

Unfortunately, that was true. They had no proof or even circumstantial evidence that Grensemann was actively involved in the porn matter, rather than just knowing about it. It was still pure speculation. "You shouldn't feel too safe," Büttner said nevertheless. "God knows you wouldn't be the first to stumble over your own arrogance."

Grensemann looked at him with a mixture of regret and contempt. It was an expression that made Büttner clench his fist in his pocket. "Your strategy has failed, Commissioner," he hissed at him. "But what would you expect from a provincial policeman."

"You told Silvia Remmers about the porn, as she told us. Allegedly you didn't know anything about it, but you wanted to confront Jesko. Did that ever happen?"

For a moment Grensemann looked irritated, but then he cleared his throat and said, "I don't know what you mean." He turned and, still leading the horse by the reins, strutted away with his head held high. Before entering the box stall, he called to him over his shoulder, "You bore me, Commissioner! Next time, why don't you send someone over to challenge my intelligence for a change, instead of insulting it?"

20

"Wow, Grensemann's really getting too big for his boots." Sebastian Hasenkrug pushed his lower lip forward and nodded, impressed. "And he literally said that to you?"

"Literally," David Büttner confirmed. "He seems to suffer from a kind of biting reflex as soon as he feels attacked. From his behaviour we can probably conclude that we were right in suspecting that he was privy to this pornography affair. But whether this knowledge will help us in our investigation is still written in the stars." He sat down at his desk and clasped his steaming mug filled with coffee with both hands. His fingers still resented the cold he had exposed them to on the cutter, they felt numb and stiff at the same time.

"Were you at least able to learn something interesting from Fokko Harms?" asked Hasenkrug.

"Nah. Apart from my realisation that he is a stubborn and at the same time mouthy dog, unfortunately not much came out of it."

"A typical East Frisian, then."

"And one who seems to enjoy staying on his cutter in bad weather and getting rained on. Such people have always been highly suspicious to me." Büttner shivered because he thought he could still feel the cold in his body, even though he had made a stop at home and treated himself to a hot shower.

Hasenkrug grinned. "It must have been a bit too much fresh air blowing around your nose on the cutter."

"Don't grin so stupidly, Hasenkrug. I know myself that this was not one of my better ideas. It would have been smarter to send you."

Hasenkrug shrugged his shoulders. "I would have liked to have seen a cutter like that up close." He looked thoughtfully out the window, behind which the Emden moat bobbed along, murky and covered in autumn leaves. "Hm. There are opportunities to book a cutter trip all along the coast, aren't there? It's supposed to be very popular with tourists. I think I should suggest such a trip to my family. I'm sure our children would enjoy it."

Büttner remained silent. Volunteering to sail on a crab cutter was so far beyond his imagination that he could not think of anything to say about his assistant's consideration.

"Did you get the impression that Fokko Harms might have had more to do with Jesko's death than fishing him out of the water?", Hasenkrug returned to her investigation.

"I don't want to rule it out, even if this is based more on my gut feeling than on him acting suspiciously in any way. But if he had something to do with the murder, I wonder why he pulled Jesko out of the North Sea and brought him ashore after he or someone else had just successfully dumped him in it."

"Right, that makes no sense." Hasenkrug sounded frustrated. "In general, we're treading water. However," he played a photo of a woman on the monitor, "I did a little research on Wiebke Storm, just as you told me to."

"Who was that again?"

"Tomke's mother and also Gina's mother's friend."

"Aha, yes, right." Büttner remembered that his stomach had sounded the alarm when she had met them at the riding stables the day before. "What is there to report about this lady?"

"She is immensely ambitious."

"Which doesn't make her a murderer."

"She comes from a very simple background," Hasenkrug continued unperturbed, "but is now a lawyer specialising in family law and building law."

"It should be a goldmine," Büttner stated.

"Indeed. I took a look at her website. She is the owner of a large and renowned law firm. More than twenty employees in two offices, in Emden and Bremen. Interestingly enough, Emden is the main office, where she usually stays. Which made sense at one point because her husband was employed there as a bank director."

"And he is not today?"

"Yes, he is. It's just that they've been divorced for almost ten years." Hasenkrug clicked further and a family photo appeared. "I found this on the internet. It shows Wiebke Storm with her ex-husband and their two daughters. We've already met Tomke, haven't we?"

"And why are you telling me all this?"

"The reason for divorce is an interesting one."

"Namely?"

"Herbert Storm – that is, the ex-husband – has or had an illegitimate child."

"Which is it? Has or had?"

"In the meantime. His wife only found out about this child long after their marriage. He had kept this part of his past from her."

"It happens in the best of families. Is there also a punch line?"

"This illegitimate child is or was Jesko Mudder."

Büttner whistled through his teeth. "Oh no! Hm. However, Jesko's mother seemed to me to belong to the rather plain sort of person. I wouldn't necessarily associate her with a bank director."

"That was probably also one of the reasons why Herbert Storm pretended throughout his life that he had nothing to do with the child. At least not officially. But at least he fulfilled his obligations and transferred money every month. However, he did so voluntarily and not because he was officially ordered to do so, because he never officially acknowledged his paternity. What he had with Antje Mudder, however, could hardly be called a relationship. The boy was probably the product of a drunken night at the shooting match. A shot, a hit, so to speak."

"That also happens in the best of families. I still don't understand what you're getting at. The wife found out about the boy at some point and drew her consequences. Probably because she felt betrayed."

"Yes, she also gave that as the reason for the divorce. But now Herbert Storm died about a week ago."

"I'm sorry for him. Do we have to assume that he died an unnatural death, or what are you getting at?"

"He died of cancer, so he is unsuspicious. However, he seems to have been seized by a guilty conscience shortly before death and declared Jesko his main heir. Since he had a not inconsiderable fortune, Jesko would have been a wealthy man. As it is, however, neither he nor his mother have heard about it yet."

"And the daughters? They should go away empty-handed?"

"Mandatory share."

"Let me guess: In the event that Jesko dies, they will become principal heiresses again."

Hasenkrug nodded. "Which gives us a motive for murder. A very classic one, in fact."

"Hm. And how does Gina Gloger fit into that?"

"Not at all. At least we haven't been able to establish a connection yet, except that she was involved with Jesko. But that doesn't give her any claim to his inheritance."

"Wiebke Storm could have confronted Jesko," Büttner pondered aloud. "There was a fistfight, Jesko fell, died … But then how did he get into the North Sea?"

"After all, Wiebke Storm is friends with one of the long-established Greetsiel fishing families," Hasenkrug said. "And the Glogers in turn …"

"… are quite thick with the Harms," Büttner continued the thought. "Which would explain why Jesko was sunk in the North Sea. But still not why they fished him out again."

After a long pause, during which Büttner had tried to tie together what they knew so far about the people involved, he asked: "Did Jesko know that Herbert Storm was his father?"

"We would have to ask his mother that. Why?"

"It would explain why there is no video of Tomke, or rather why Jesko never tried to hook up with her or even get her into bed."

Hasenkrug nodded. "In that case, Jesko would have known that Tomke was his half-sister. But if Tomke didn't know the other way round: what reason did he have not to tell her? Jesko was not someone who would have cared about the sensitivities of a Herbert Storm. The way he was, it's more likely that he would have blown Storm's cover long ago with much fanfare."

"How do you know Tomke doesn't know about it?"

"That's right, we haven't asked them about that. We should do that." Hasenkrug scribbled a note in his pad.

"But it's also possible that Jesko kept the secret for his mother's sake," Büttner objected. "Somewhere even a Jesko Mudder must have had a soft spot, even if he did everything he could to hide it." He sighed. "But no matter how you look at it, Gina's murder still doesn't fit the picture."

A short laugh could be heard from the anteroom, then the door swung open and Marieke came in. Today she was leaning on her walking aids again, which seemed to make her visibly exert herself. Sweat was standing on her forehead and her face was much paler than the day before.

"Phew. It's good to be here at last." Without having greeted her colleagues, she slumped down on a chair with a groan, her face contorted in obvious pain. It also sounded tortured when she said in an unusually thin voice: "I think I really should slow down a bit."

"My talking," growled Büttner.

Marieke waved her hand. "Nah, nah, I don't mean work." She gratefully accepted a bottle of water that Hasenkrug handed her and emptied half of it in one go. Then she wiped her mouth with her forearm and said, "I've been training under Jelka's guidance for two hours until just now. She admonished me that it was too much, but I still wanted to go on. I should have listened to her. This is how slowly I should know my limits. That's probably why she let me do it. If you don't want to listen, you have to feel, or something."

"Above all, you should have taken a longer break before coming here," Büttner said reprovingly.

"Yes, maybe." She eyed her crutches with an almost desperate look. "Now I'm actually wishing for my wheelchair. Crazy, isn't it?"

Hasenkrug jumped up and reached for his car key, which was lying on the desk. "The wheelchair is at your house, isn't it? I'll get it for you." He held out his hand, which probably meant that she should give him her flat key.

"Nah, thanks, I'm fine, Sebastian," she waved it off. "I'm only here because I found out something that might interest you. You should stay here for that. As soon as I get rid of what I have to say, I'll be on my way home. I promise. I've already called my mother, she'll pick me up in half an hour. She'll bring my wheelchair with her."

"She doesn't have to," Hasenkrug insisted. "I can drive you after all. Or someone else from the colleagues."

"Nah, it's fine. My mother is out on the town anyway." Marieke laughed. "I'll have to listen to a telling off from her, too. She doesn't like it at all that I'm already putting so much time and energy into work."

"Now you're just saying." Büttner also lacked any understanding for this, as much as he could use Marieke's help. They had had to worry about her for too long for him to simply overlook the fact that she was putting her weakened body through far too much now. However, he knew her well enough to know that she would not leave until she had shared her latest findings with them. "All right, Marieke, get on with it!" he therefore urged her. "But as soon as you realise that it's getting to you, stop immediately."

"You got it, boss." She sat up in her chair. "Now, I don't know how thoroughly you've looked at the men who are on the client list of Jesko's porn site." She looked questioningly from one to the other.

"You tell us," Hasenkrug said with a shrug.

"Then please play the list on the monitor, Sebastian."

No sooner said than done. Only a little later, an Excel spreadsheet appeared on the screen.

"It's still unbelievable how many names there are," Büttner said, shaking his head. "Wiebke Storm will get a lot of customers when the vice squad has worked its way through the men."

"For that to happen, Vice would first have to prove the men knowingly accessed illegally produced videos," Hasenkrug said.

Marieke looked questioningly from one to the other, but Büttner waved it off. "Not so important." He could still inform her of Hasenkrug's findings on Wiebke Storm in due course. "Which one of the sex-hungry guys did you pick, Marieke?"

"Heiko Jürgens-Schmaler."

One click of the mouse from Hasenkrug, and this name showed itself to them on the screen, marked in red.

"What about him?", Büttner wanted to know.

"Heiko Jürgens-Schmaler. Forty-one years old, married, three children, credit-financed home, youth coach in the local football club, chairman of the parents' association at his twin daughters' primary school."

"How nice for him," Büttner growled. "At least until his wife finds out what he's up to when she's not looking. But what does he of all people have to do with our case?"

"He works in the Lower Saxony Ministry of Education in Hanover in a fairly high position. In the school department."

Büttner was on the edge of his seat, and his assistant didn't look as if he spontaneously knew what Marieke was getting at either.

"Oh dear," said Hasenkrug only seconds later. "I think I know what you … Oops, that would really be …!" He leaned back in his chair and ran both hands through his hair. "Well, if that's what I think you're trying to tell us, then … wow! Then he'd have a real problem."

"Would someone like to let me share?" grumbled Büttner. "I … oh." A flash of inspiration came to him now, too, and he looked from one to the other with wide eyes. "You're not, by any chance, making a connection between the accidental graduation of … what were their names?"

"Sanna and Lisa," Marieke and Hasenkrug said as if from the same mouth. "Yes, exactly," Marieke then confirmed his assumption. "It's still pure speculation, but somehow the A-level exams must have found their way to them prematurely."

"He can be blackmailed." Büttner nodded.

"So he might have felt compelled to leak the exams. It's unlikely that he did this without a corresponding," Hasenkrug drew inverted commas in the air, "request."

"For which none other than Jesko Mudder comes into question," Büttner added, "because he was the only one who knew who enjoyed his porn."

"Unless Christopher Grensemann actually had access to the data," Hasenkrug said. "Hopefully our IT department will find that out in time."

"All the more reason to put some steam under the kettle of our IT people," said Büttner. "And who better to do that than you, Hasenkrug."

"I'll get right on it later."

"If it really was the case that this …" Büttner leaned forward to read the name on the screen better, "Heiko Jürgens-Schmaler punctured the exams on Jesko, then …"

"… Jesko probably did it to get back at Sanna and Lisa," Marieke finished the sentence. "For the video that not only cost him his job, but made him the laughing stock of the internet community for several weeks."

"Then it's probably time to send this Mr Jürgens-Schmaler a message to encourage him to have a chat," Büttner said. "I could imagine that he would rather talk to us than have the public prosecutor's office take up the matter."

"Which, however, can hardly be prevented," Hasenkrug pointed out.

"Of course not," Büttner agreed with him. "But he doesn't know that."

21

Around two hours later, David Büttner put the phone back on the hook. "Good, that's done," he sighed. "Now we just have to check his alibi. It shouldn't be too difficult to prove or disprove that Jürgens-Schmaler was on a business trip in Bavaria when Gina and Jesko were murdered. The ministerial official is therefore unlikely to be the murderer."

"Unless Jürgens-Schmaler hired someone to carry out the murders," Sebastian Hasenkrug, who had listened to the telephone conversation over the loudspeaker, said. "But I don't think so, because he doesn't seem like the type.

"Büttner was also convinced: "As afraid as he was that his regular porn consumption would become known to his wife and the ministry, he would not have had the nerve to carry out a murder contract. "Apparently he didn't even know the name of the blackmailer, but sent the exam documents to an anonymous e-mail address, as he could credibly assure us. So how could he have known who was behind this blackmail?"

"He also assumed that the blackmailer, presumably Jesko, wanted the exam papers for himself," Hasenkrug added. "It was no coincidence that he asked us several times to look for the blackmailer among the school-leavers. He didn't even know at which Lower Saxony grammar school the cheating had taken place, let alone whether anyone had been caught cheating. No idea whether we can believe him."

"Anyway, Jürgens-Schmaler is out with it. At least as far as the murder investigation is concerned. Our colleagues will take care of everything else. I wouldn't want to be in his shoes."

Hasenkrug shrugged his shoulders. "My sympathy is limited. After all, no one forced him to watch the porn, even if he was constantly tempted to portray himself as a victim. Which is something I particularly like in a case like this." He looked at his screen. "A message just came in from Chris Bäumler." Immediately he slapped his hands together with a "Yep". "Okay, now we know for sure. The exam that cost Sanna and Lisa their Abitur was found on Jesko's computer. Well hidden and password-protected and therefore not to be found at first go. But our IT team cracked the file. That should make it certain that Jesko is the author of the whole mess."

"Very good, that brings us a good step forward. So now we can tackle the next step." Büttner stood up and went into the anteroom. "Mrs Weniger? Have the witnesses arrived yet?"

The secretary made a head movement towards the door. "Sanna and Lisa are waiting outside in the corridor. They were quite surprised when I called them and asked them to come. Accordingly, they arrived here nervous. But, well, it's not every day you get a summons from the criminal police. And so spontaneously."

The young women were not only nervous, as Büttner noticed immediately afterwards, but apparently completely finished with their nerves. At least that was true of Lisa, who sat slumped over in tears, her body shaken by sobs. Sanna, on the other hand, stared at the opposite wall with a petrified expression, as if she had to drill two holes into it with her eyes.

When Büttner joined them, they both flinched in equal measure and looked at him as if they expected to be led to the scaffold by him. He wondered what had upset them so much.

"Please," Lisa sniffled barely audibly, "please, Commissioner. I didn't want this. I certainly didn't want it."

"We know it was not intentional," Büttner tried to reassure them.

"Yes?" A glimmer of hope flashed in Lisa's reddened eyes. She looked at Sanna with a hint of relief, but she only pressed her lips together and avoided her gaze.

"Well, please come with us. We have a few more questions for you."

Sanna and Lisa followed him into the office and, at a prompting gesture from Hasenkrug, took a seat on a chair opposite Büttner's desk.

"So," Büttner prompted her. "Then tell us. We've learned that you were excluded from the examination because of cheating. Why don't you tell us how that came about?"

"It was awful," Lisa sobbed. "We … we were just about to start writing our maths exam. The assignments were already distributed. And all of a sudden … all of a sudden …" Her voice broke as she slumped down again in a crying fit, hands in front of her face.

"Suddenly the director came in and checked all the tables," Sanna picked up the thread again at Büttner's prompting look. She, too, had horror written all over her face as she continued after a deep breath: "I ... we ... well ... of course we were pretty angry when we found out that they had put the paper with the solutions under our desks ..." She fell silent and narrowed her eyes. "Shit, man," she said barely audibly. When she raised her head again, tears ran down her cheeks too. "I mean, how could they think we'd be so stupid as to bring the solutions to school then, too?"

"They've asked us a thousand times how we got the assignments along with the solutions," Lisa sobbed. "Over and over again they asked us that." She raised her hands in a helpless gesture and then lowered them again powerlessly. "But what were we supposed to say? We didn't know ourselves how it happened and ... and who shoved them under our desks."

Büttner waited, but neither of them made any move to say anything else. They seemed far too caught up in their unpleasant memories. So he let them be, so that they could collect themselves. Still, he wondered why, after all these months, they were still so upset when the subject came up. Or was it not so much the unsuccessful graduation as the death of their friend that upset them so much?

"Then when we found out that Gina was behind it all, there ..." Sanna bit her lips and stared at the ceiling. "I ... we ... I still don't know why she did it."

"Gina?" Büttner leaned over the desk and stared at her. "You think Gina smuggled the solutions under your desk?" He gave Hasenkrug, who looked a little confused, a meaningful look. He, however, seemed to be deep in thought. He was probably also trying to make sense of what he had just said. "May I ask what made you think it was Gina?"

"Jesko told us."

"Excuse me?" Büttner had no idea how to classify this information. Was it possible that Jesko had told Gina about the porn website and that she had then blackmailed the ministry official? But what motive could she have had for messing up her friends' exams? And besides, what was the exam doing on Jesko's computer?

"When exactly did Jesko tell you?"

"Last week," Lisa whispered.

"The written exams were in February," Büttner said. "So why should he only come out with this alleged knowledge in November?"

"I don't know. We were at a party. He was drunk. Well, and that's when he just said it. I think he was stressed out with Gina."

Büttner remembered the statement of his colleague Eiko Harms, who had had the impression that Gina had been afraid the night before her death. Had it been because of Jesko? And if so, what had he threatened her with?

"And you believed him? Just like that?"

"Nah, of course not. But he showed us the exam and the solutions. He had found them on Gina's computer. And they had also been printed out from there the day before our exam."

"Did he claim," growled Büttner.

"Nah. He showed us. Jesko knew his way around computers. He knew where to look. It was Gina's computer and it was her printer," Sanna insisted.

"What was he doing on Gina's computer?"

All he got in reply was a shrug of the shoulders.

"Why should Gina have done that to you?", Hasenkrug now spoke up again. "Did you have a fight or something?"

Sanna and Lisa shook their heads. "No," Sanna replied. "Gina was blatantly ambitious. But we were much better at maths than she was. Maybe she just wanted to … Nah, I don't know why she did that. Actually, she wasn't like that. We asked ourselves that a thousand times, of course."

"That's why we wanted to know from her," Lisa whispered barely audibly, while tears continued to run down her face. She had long since stopped trying to avoid them.

In view of her deep despair, Büttner couldn't shake the uneasy feeling that there was more to this story than a screwed-up exam. "And what did Gina say?"

"She just laughed and said that we shouldn't say shit like that. And that we had only ourselves to blame."

"When was that?"

Lisa and Sanna glanced at each other, both eyes now filled with naked fear.

"We … well, when we met her."

"When exactly?"

They exchanged another look, then both shook their heads. "We don't really know any more," Sanna breathed.

Büttner swallowed hard as he realised what the stammering meant. "It was Monday evening, wasn't it?"

"M-Monday? Why M-Monday?"

"You went to see Gina at Jesko's flat on Monday night to confront her. Is that right?"

Lisa burst into loud sobs, but Sanna, after a long silence in which she visibly struggled with herself, said: "Jesko let us in. He … he said that Gina was in the bathroom. Then he left."

Büttner expelled his breath noisily. "He left?"

"Yes. He was in a hurry. Wanted to go somewhere."

"And you stayed?"

"Yes."

There was now an almost unbearable tension in the office. It slowly dawned on Büttner where the deep despair of the two women came from, and he felt little desire to have this suspicion confirmed. Hasenkrug seemed to feel the same way, because he nervously slid back and forth on his chair and avoided catching his gaze, as if by doing so he could undo everything that was about to happen.

"We waited for Gina in the kitchen, but she didn't come," Lisa whispered. "I … I wish we had just left again. But I … I was so angry with her and so … so disappointed."

"We had to confront her," Sanna explained barely louder, "now that we finally knew the truth. Otherwise we would have choked on our anger."

"You went in search of her?" Büttner noticed himself that his voice sounded occupied.

"Yes. We found her in the bathroom like Jesko had said. She was lying in the bathtub. She was holding a squeaky duck that looked like a fairy. With a magic wand and all."

"How did Gina react when you suddenly stood in front of her?"

"She has … she has …" Lisa gave Sanna an uncertain look, who nodded in response. "She acted as if nothing was wrong. She smiled at us, like she always did when we met. She said 'hi' and 'what's up' and like … yeah, like everything was cool between us." Remembering the situation, her voice suddenly became shrill, her eyes began to flash angrily. "And that really pissed me off," she abruptly shouted into the room. "I mean, how could she lie in the tub with her stupid squeaky duck and act like everything was cool?! She had messed up our future! She can't pretend that everything is cool!"

"What happened then?" asked Hasenkrug.

"I … I totally freaked out," Sanna said. "I was yelling at her, what was she thinking, pretending for months that nothing had happened. All this time she had been pretending to feel sorry for us. She constantly asked us if we wanted to do something, go riding together, whatever. She said that distraction would do us good. And we believed her that she was doing this because she was our friend. Because she believes us that we didn't cheat on purpose."

"Yet she was the one who got us into shit, and on purpose," Lisa added in a quivering voice. "And then she lay there in her fucking foam bath and acted like she didn't know what we wanted her to do, why we were so pissed off. "Hey, ladies," she mimicked Gina's tone, "what have you been smoking to be so weird? Now chill, okay?!" Lisa, now shaking all over, closed her eyes for a moment. "Then she took foam and blew it in our direction. Like it was all just a game."

Büttner sighed inwardly. He was sure that it had really

only been a game for Gina and that she had only wanted to reassure her friends. "So what?" he asked, although he didn't want to hear it.

"I was so angry that I rushed towards her and pushed her head under the water," Sanna croaked, as if suddenly struggling with hoarseness. "Over and over again. I was … like in a frenzy. It … felt so good to finally be able to let off steam. And all of a sudden …" Her eyes reflected horror. "All of a sudden, Gina was very still. She didn't move anymore."

"And you?", Büttner turned to Lisa. "What did you do?"

"Nothing. I … didn't do anything."

"That means you didn't try to stop it either, even though it was obvious that Sanna was just losing it and Gina was fighting for her life?"

Lisa shook her head. "I didn't do anything." Barely audible, she added after a few seconds, "But Gina deserved it. She ruined our future." She lifted her gaze and looked Büttner straight in the eye. "Didn't she? She deserved it for that."

"No," Büttner replied after a deep breath, "she certainly didn't. No one deserves to die that way." He paused meaningfully. "And certainly not if you haven't done anything to anyone."

Sanna and Lisa stared at him wide-eyed, and Lisa cried out angrily, "But she has …"

"Nothing done," Hasenkrug cut her off.

"Didn't you listen to us?" croaked Sanna, struggling for composure. "Gina gave us the retreat …"

Büttner hit the desk with the flat of his hand. "That's

enough!" He had to collect himself before he said calmly with effort, "Now listen to me! We are sure that Gina had nothing to do with this. All the facts are against it." He looked at Sanna and Lisa, who were staring at him in disbelief, until they avoided his gaze. "It wasn't her who foisted the retreat on you. It was Jesko. Surely you remember the unflattering video you posted of him on the net that caused quite a stir?"

Two pairs of oversized eyes, reflecting comprehension, stared at him.

"But Gina still knew about it," came almost like a cry for help from Lisa, while Sanna just sat there dumbfounded. "She knew about all this. She must have known!"

Büttner shook his head. "No. There is nothing to suggest that Gina knew about it. She was just … your friend."

22

"Shit," Sebastian Hasenkrug summed up what he had just experienced in one word. He threw his biros, on the end of which he had been clicking for minutes, into the room in a fit of anger, where it shattered on the floor. David Büttner nodded silently.

After Sanna and Lisa had been taken away, there was a melancholy mood in the office that could not be shaken off so easily. So they just let it be for a few minutes and sipped their coffee that Mrs Weniger had brought them. She too had remained silent, just shaking her head again and again in bewilderment.

Before a colleague had taken care of the women, they had learned from Sanna and Lisa that Jesko had returned to the flat only a few minutes after Gina's death. Grasping the situation, he had stared at them both in horror and fear and then stormed out again without a word. Whether he had ever realised how big his part in the disaster was, they would probably never find out.

"We then called Christopher," Sanna had said. "He said we had to get rid of Gina because there were too many traces of us in the flat."

When Büttner asked if it had occurred to them to call the police, Lisa had shrugged her shoulders. "I don't think we could think at all. Christopher came and we just did what he said. He said if we dressed Gina and threw her in the dock, no one would ever know she drowned in the bathtub. Then it would look like an accident and no one would ask questions."

In the meantime, a patrol car was on its way to the Grensemanns to take Christopher into custody as well. Büttner was not yet able to say when he would be ready to talk to him, because of course it was foreseeable that the arrogant snob would deny everything. At the moment, Büttner lacked both the desire and the nerves to get involved in such an interrogation. So Grensemann would have to wait in the interrogation room – which would give him enough time to think, as Büttner stated not without a certain satisfaction.

"We are still missing Jesko's murderer," Hasenkrug broke the silence after what felt like an eternity. "Unfortunately, there are so many motives why someone could have wanted to kill him that it would be a huge task to go through all the potential suspects again."

"I know I'm not supposed to say it," Büttner growled. "But after everything we've been able to find out about Jesko, my motivation to find his murderer is sinking …"

Hasenkrug stopped him with a gesture. "You'd better not say it, boss. I know what you mean anyway."

"… towards zero," Büttner nevertheless completed his sentence. Sometimes what had to be said simply had to be said.

"Whatever," Hasenkrug said after clearing his throat. "As I said, we probably won't get around it …" His smartphone began to ring. "It's Marieke," he stated immediately.

Büttner rolled his eyes. "Let her rest!"

"Marieke?" Hasenkrug had taken the call. "Wait, I'll put you on speaker."

"Howdy, everybody," she greeted. "How many of you are there?"

"Just the boss and me."

"You should take it easy, Marieke," Büttner grumbled.

"I'm lying on the sofa at home, a hot water bottle under my aching back, a cat on my swollen feet, a cup of tea next to me. You can't take it any easier than that."

Büttner made an unwilling sound, but refrained from further admonishments. They were of no avail anyway.

"Okay, guys. Anything new?"

"Indeed." Hasenkrug told her about Sanna and Lisa.

"Awesome," was Marieke's reaction. She was silent for a few seconds, only a few deep breaths could be heard. But then she said, "Well, it is what it is. I've come across something. Where are you with the porn website? I mean, do you know the identities of all the women on there by now?"

"Not yet," said Hasenkrug. "It's undoubtedly too delicate a matter to go public with pictures, and we haven't got the green light for it yet. Victim protection, if you know what I mean. As long as we haven't informed the women personally and our investigations …"

"Yes, yes, all right, Sebastian, that's enough explanation. I just wanted to know if you had all names."

"No. At least we haven't got a final list yet."

"Okay. Then I have a name for you now. Fasten your seatbelts!"

"Um…"

"Surely our IT has the possibility to check whether Eiko Harms has watched the videos in the last few days?" asked Marieke. "He was on duty in the last few days, wasn't he?"

"As far as I know, yes. Why?"

"Does IT have the option, or doesn't it?" insisted Marieke.

"I assume so, yes."

"Then please let the boys have a look right away. It's really important."

Hasenkrug gave Büttner a questioning look, whereupon he nodded. "Tell them to hurry up," he growled.

"Tuesday afternoon," Hasenkrug reported only a few minutes later. "One video after the other. And the following days he logged on several times, but only to the video of a certain Chiara, whose real name is Talea."

Büttner grimaced in disgust. "Someone seems to have taken a liking to what is being shown."

"Probably the opposite." Marieke sounded tense. "Where is Eiko now? Is he on duty?"

"I don't know."

"Then please consult the duty roster," she said impatiently.

Hasenkrug let his fingers slide over the keyboard, a little later he said, "Eiko's not on duty today."

"Okay. Or rather not okay. I'll get right back to you."

Before Büttner and Hasenkrug could say anything back, she had hung up.

"What was that?" asked Büttner perplexed.

"Looks like she found out something about this Talea." Again Hasenkrug's fingers flew over the keyboard, he looked intently at the screen. "I just wonder what this has to do with Eiko Harms."

"Then let's hope Marieke tells us soon …" Büttner faltered as Hasenkrug uttered a suppressed curse. "What's up?"

"I think I know what Marieke was getting at," Hasenkrug enlightened him in a thin voice. "Eiko has a sister. She is seventeen years old and her name is …"

"Talea." Büttner groaned and closed his eyes for a moment. "I was all for releasing him from duty right away, but apparently his direct superiors saw no reason to do so."

Hasenkrug's phone again announced a call from Marieke. He answered with the words: "Talea is Eiko's sister, isn't she?"

"Yes."

"Have you been able to find out where Eiko is right now?"

"Yes. He went out in the cutter."

"Well, then, in the foreseeable future …"

"Nothing is good at all," Marieke impatiently interrupted him. "Eiko has obviously gone out on his own. He made one of their cutters ready tonight without coordinating it with his father or anyone else. And he certainly didn't intend to go crabbing. Attempts have already been made to locate him, but apparently he switched off all the relevant equipment on board as soon as he passed the Leysiel lock. The coastguard has been alerted. But unless he happens to be spotted by another ship, it will be damn difficult to find him."

"He has to dock somewhere," Hasenkrug said. "He needs fuel and provisions. I'll see to it right away that all the North Sea ports are informed. And preferably those on the Baltic as well, in case he decides to cross the Kiel Canal."

"That should be an endless number," groaned Büttner.

"Well, it's not like we have to handwrite a letter to every harbour master, put a stamp on it and take it to the post office," Marieke replied. "I don't know if you knew, boss, but we live in the digital age."

"So Eiko Harms is on the run," Büttner decided to ignore Marieke's point. "He took one of the cutters to make a run for it because he knew it wouldn't be long before we caught on to him."

Hasenkrug nodded in agreement. "His motive should be clear. First Jesko steals his girlfriend, and then he has to find out that Jesko not only seduced his underage sister, but also threw her to some lecher. I guess that was enough to make him want to kill."

"Do we have the data of the fugitive cutter?" Büttner asked Marieke.

"Colleagues are inquiring about them with Fokko Harms right now."

Büttner stood up. "Well, let's go to the Harms family and see what else we can find out. Maybe the prodigal son has told someone what the destination of his excursion is and what he plans to do there."

23

"Why does the boy do that?" whined Bärbel Harms. "I don't understand. What's he doing out there all alone with that cutter?" Despite her concern, which was easy to read on her face, she had taken the liberty of brewing a fresh East Frisian tea. She put sugar cubes in the cups and poured the hot tea on them so that it crackled comfortably while the autumn rain pelted the windows and the wind made the shutters rattle. Then, using a traditional swan spoon, she enveloped the tea in a billowing cloud of cream. "And what does all this have to do with the police? I really don't understand."

Büttner and Hasenkrug were sitting in the kitchen of the Harms' traditional Frisian house, which Büttner liked much better than the Glogers' modern building. He had always imagined the home of a fishing family to be like the Harms'. A little quaint and cramped, with lots of stuff and knick-knacks everywhere and oil paintings on the walls. These mostly showed a gloomy, threatening North Sea and sailors bravely facing the elemental forces.

"Eiko will surely be back soon. Or what do you think, Fokko?" Bärbel Harms turned to her husband, who was sitting there smoking a pipe and only gave a growl. He didn't seem to be able to understand the situation either, his eyes sometimes flickering with anger and then with concern.

"How often have you seen Eiko in the last few days, that is, after Gina was found dead?" inquired Büttner. He took a piece of honey cake from the plate that Bärbel Harms had cut open and was now passing around.

"Not often," Harms growled. "He usually had a shift at the police station. And besides, he doesn't live here anymore. I only really get to see him when we go out on the cutter together."

"And you?", Büttner turned to Harms' wife.

"Oh, Eiko usually comes in once a day to get a cup of tea. He's always worried about me, you know." She patted her hip. "Been having trouble with my joints for a while. You don't get any younger."

"Did you have the impression that Eiko was different than usual in the last few days?" asked Hasenkrug after he had brought his cup to his mouth. "Mmh, the tea is really quite excellent."

"Well, he was sad, of course. Because of Gina." Bärbel Harms sighed from the bottom of her heart. "But you can understand that. How terrible it all is – for Amke and Tjark, too, what Gina's parents are – you don't want to think about it, it's all so terrible."

"Apart from the mourning for Gina, Eiko was like anything else?" asked Büttner.

"No," Fokko Harms spoke up. But that was all he said.

"What was he like then?"

"Different."

"I see." Büttner felt a certain impatience rising within

him. "And how exactly did this Different express himself? In more than one word, if possible."

"Rather quieter."

Okay, that was still twice as many words as before.

"But now you could also tell us why you are here," Harms unexpectedly spoke in one complete sentence. He wouldn't start chatting, would he?

Büttner wondered which catastrophe they should confront Eiko's parents with first. With the fact that Eiko was strongly suspected of having killed Jesko? Or would it be appropriate to first point out to them the pornographic film in which their underage daughter involuntarily played a leading role?

He decided on the latter, because it would make their later expressed suspicion that Eiko might have something to do with Jesko's death even more plausible. It was to be feared that this would in no way alleviate the parents' horror and pain, but Büttner did not know how that could be done at all under the circumstances. What he had to say would always be a shock, no matter how one twisted and turned the matter.

"We would like to show you something," he said. He nodded at Hasenkrug, whereupon the latter's facial features tightened. His assistant also clearly did not feel comfortable confronting the parents with the video.

Hasenkrug had a tablet with him for this purpose, on which he called up the corresponding file. "I'm sorry to have to show this to you," he said before turning the tablet so that the two of them could watch the film without any problems.

It took only a few seconds for something to fundamentally change in the parents' posture. At first Fokko Harms had sat stoically, but now his whole body tensed and his facial expression reflected bewilderment. Bärbel Harms, on the other hand, put her hands in front of her face and began to shake all over.

"W-why are you showing us this?" she croaked. "We … don't want to see this."

Fokko Harms, on the other hand, said nothing, but clenched his fists and stared at Büttner and Hasenkrug as if they were the authors of this video. Instinctively, Büttner pressed himself deeper into the cushions of the corner bench on which he was sitting.

Hasenkrug also seemed to sense that the fisherman was about to explode. He quickly withdrew the tablet and switched it off, then said emphatically matter-of-factly: "This video was recorded by Jesko Mudder without your daughter's knowledge and offered on the internet for …", he swallowed hard, "… for sale."

Harms' body reared up, his gaze suddenly that of a cornered animal. He brought his fists crashing down on the table, so that the dishes clinked and the tea spilled over the rims of the cups. But he still said nothing, only a gurgling sound escaped his throat.

In view of the father's reaction, Büttner was sure that Jesko Mudder's life could not have been saved by now at the latest. "Eiko has seen this video," he hurried to add an explanation. "On his service computer. Unfortunately, it is to be feared that it was he who killed Jesko. Not least because he was already … because of Gina."

Again Harms' hands thundered on the table, and now he also found his speech again. "He's right, the boy! I hope he showed him right! This piece of shit has already done far too much damage. Jesko's got no business on this earth floor anymore." He puffed like a startled ox. "Too bad the scumbag is already dead. I would have been only too happy to claw my fingers down his throat until he made no more sound." To punctuate his words, he made a corresponding movement with his hands.

"Did …" Bärbel Harms pointed to the tablet in Hasenkrug's hand with a lame movement. "Did Jesko do that to Gina too? Did he … did he kill her because of that?"

"Jesko didn't kill Gina," Büttner explained. *At least not directly,* he added in his mind.

But these words did not soften Fokko Harms at all. Rather, he now seemed intent on breaking something. Avoiding his gaze, which was flashing with rage, Büttner fervently hoped that the fisherman was not toying with the idea of venting his anger on him of all people. Because if the fisherman's steel fist landed in his face, he would certainly not have to look forward to tomorrow.

"I don't believe you!", Harms yelled into the room.

Oh, dear.

The fisherman had jumped up. His chair fell to the floor behind him, the table and the dishes shook, the tea poured out of the pot and cups onto the oilcloth, leaving several laughs in its wake. The teapot warmer with the burning tea light began to sway dangerously, but thankfully remained standing.

"You're just saying that so that I … so that I … uaaaaah!"

Harms, who no longer seemed to know where to put his anger, grabbed the teapot and hurled it against the wall. The porcelain shattered into a thousand pieces, the tea splashed in a torrent onto the corner bench. Thank God, however, it did not soak the cushions on which Büttner and Hasenkrug had been sitting, but the other side. Thus the commissioners got quite a few splashes that burned into their palms as well as their faces, but at least they were spared a complete hot shower.

Büttner saw Hasenkrug frantically typing on his smartphone, which Harms, in his rage, fortunately did not notice. Instead, he swept all the dishes off the table, which resulted in a loud clattering and clanging.

There was no stopping the fisherman. He smashed whatever came between his fingers. His wife had let herself sink from her chair to the floor and was cowering, arms folded protectively over her head, in the middle of a pool of tea under the table, whimpering.

"Why don't you see to it that you stop him!" Büttner murmured to his assistant while he tried to protect his face from any splinters that were flying through the kitchen. In his place on the corner bench, from which there was no escape for him, he felt increasingly uncomfortable. It was surely only a matter of time before the crazed fisherman would also set his sights on her, especially since there was hardly anything else in the kitchen that he had not already smashed.

As Harms stumbled in their direction as if in a frenzy, Hasenkrug slid towards the edge of the corner bench. The fisherman, holding a chair above his head, staggered towards one of the transom windows, took a swing – and, as Hasenkrug tripped him up, hit the floor belly-first and hard lengthways in the next moment. The chair crashed full force against the white-plastered wall, shattered with a crunch, and Büttner watched in horror as several sharp splinters of wood bore into the fisherman's shoulders and neck in the next moment.

Harms' ensuing screams, which seemed to come more from his anger than from the pain, did not bode well, but before he even had a chance to get back on his feet, Hasenkrug was already kneeling on his back, yanking his arms back and making the handcuffs click.

Harms cursed under him and kicked his legs so that Hasenkrug had a hard time keeping the colossus under control.

Büttner was all the more relieved when the door flew open the next moment, four colleagues in uniform assessed the situation in seconds and put an end to the whole commotion immediately.

"Wow, what a battlefield!" marvelled a paramedic who entered the kitchen a little later with a colleague. He ran up to Büttner. "Are you all right, Commissioner?"

Büttner waved it off. "Yes, yes, there's nothing wrong with me." He pointed at Bärbel Harms, who was still cowering under the table and could not be persuaded to crawl out from under it even by a uniformed colleague who spoke to her in a soft voice. "Take care of her." Then he pointed to Fokko Harms, who, held in check by Hasenkrug and two other colleagues, was now lying on the ground whimpering like a child. "Look at his injuries, too. But treat him with care. He has enough to cope with already." He gave his colleagues a penetrating look. "That goes for you too."

Büttner struggled up from the bench, but had to support himself briefly on the table when his knees threatened to give way under him. The shock was deep and he would have to give himself a few minutes to digest it.

"Oh, by the way," a colleague spoke up as Büttner and Hasenkrug immediately headed for the exit. "I don't know if you've heard yet. Shortly before Helgoland, the coast guard has picked up a Greetsiel fishing boat. It seems to be the one we are looking for."

Büttner paused in his movement. "Were they able to arrest the skipper?"

The colleague shook his head. "There was no one on board. The barge was completely abandoned in the North Sea.

"Oh, fuck," Hasenkrug said, while a lump formed in Büttner's throat that was so big he couldn't get a word out. This case could not have ended any worse!

He glanced back at the Harms, who were frozen in their movement at their colleague's words. Of course, it was also clear to them what an abandoned Greetsiel cutter off Helgoland meant.

Büttner felt tears welling up in his eyes at the suddenly almost soulless look in Eiko's mother's eyes, but he swallowed them.

"I'm … I'm very sorry," he murmured before stepping out into the rain and storm.

24

Christoph Grensemann had spent long hours in the interrogation room before David Büttner and Sebastian Hasenkrug joined him after their return from Greetsiel. Nevertheless, he seemed to have lost none of his arrogance, for he looked at them with the arrogant expression they now knew so well about him.

Even though Büttner would have preferred to call it a day after everything they had experienced that day, he was in the right mood to finally clip the young man's wings. And he did so on behalf of Jesko Mudder, whom they could no longer prosecute. The fact that one man with his intrigues had been able to bring so much useless suffering to so many innocent people … Büttner still couldn't get his head around it.

"Moin." Büttner slammed a stack of files on the table that he had brought along especially for this purpose. Such a gesture rarely failed to have the desired effect on the other person, and so he observed with satisfaction that Grensemann also flinched briefly.

Büttner and Hasenkrug sat down.

"You're not doing that to me! Not that!" Grensemann nagged at him the next moment with his index finger extended. Apparently he had decided to take over from now on. "I want to see my lawyer right now! Letting me rot here for hours …"

"We'll finish faster if you just hold your breath." Büttner had to strain to remain calm. He glanced at his wristwatch. "Believe me, I too would rather be at home right now than dealing with you. But unfortunately you had to spoil my end of the day."

Grensemann seemed to want to flare up again, already taking a deep breath of pleasure, but then he seemed to think of a new tactic. He stretched his upper body, lifted his chin and eyed Büttner from above, letting his disdainful gaze roam over his not exactly slender figure. "Well, just tell me in three words what this is all about and you can finally get down to what you seem to do best."

"You are under arrest," Büttner gladly complied with this request. He enjoyed seeing Grensemann's features derail in response.

"You will be pleased to hear that we have also already prepared a place for you to sleep for the night," he took advantage of the pause that arose. "Unfortunately, I am obliged to point out that you do not have to say anything that incriminates yourself. Still, a little tip: a confession always goes down well with the judge. Well?"

Grensemann quickly recovered from his fright, for he now put his head back and began to laugh artificially. "My God, Büttner, you almost got me now." He wagged his index finger around. "Maybe I did underestimate you, you old bluffer!" He became serious again, propped himself up with his forearm and bent over the table. "Which

I don't really believe, though, because it's not like me to be wrong in my assessments."

"Then I'm sorry to have to shake this article of faith, Mr Grensemann," Büttner replied after a deep sigh. "Because your assessment that our esteemed forensic expert would miss the fact that Gina did not drown in the harbour basin but in the bathtub was definitely a wrong one."

Grensemann's lower jaw dropped for a moment, but he quickly got his facial muscles back under control. He snorted derisively. "Well, whether it's a dock or a bathtub, the bottom line is the same for Gina, isn't it?" He tugged at his shirt collar. "But why are you telling me this anyway? I don't quite see what it has to do with me."

For the first time, Hasenkrug joined in the conversation after sighing and glancing at the clock on the wall. "I guess Sanna and Lisa are already enjoying their supper in the prison dining room. It would be a shame if you missed yours, wouldn't it? It's so hard to sleep when you're hungry."

"S-anna and Lisa?" stammered Grensemann, visibly perplexed. "W-why?"

"Tell us," said Büttner. "Your tip to them about dumping Gina's body in the harbour basin was a really shitty one. The word cover-up isn't exactly what makes a judge's heart beat faster." Now it was he who leaned forward. "Between you and me, Grensemann, you didn't help those two cover up the killing without ulterior motives, did you? Will you tell us your plan?"

"I … uh…" Grensemann's gaze flickered nervously back and forth between you. He seemed to want to assess what they knew and what they didn't.

"Was it about blackmail?" asked Hasenkrug. "I guess Lisa and Sanna won't go easy on you now. A good starting position to confide in us, don't you think?"

Grensemann swallowed hard. "I … I want to speak to my lawyer."

"I guess that's a definite yes then." Büttner nodded. "I figured Sanna wouldn't be with a guy like you by choice at all." He gathered up his papers and stood up. "Anyway, you can tell us everything else tomorrow. For example, what role you played in Jesko Mudder's porno distribution."

Before leaving the interrogation room, he turned to his uniformed colleague who was standing guard at the door: "It is quite possible that Mr Grensemann has lost his appetite. But please make sure he gets his dinner anyway. After all, you don't want to be accused of anything."

With an audible sigh, David Büttner put his smartphone back on the kitchen table. He had just received an e-mail with an attachment from Sebastian Hasenkrug. According to it, Eiko Harms had left a suicide note in which he not only announced his suicide on the open sea, but also confessed to having beaten Jesko Mudder to death in a fit of unbridled rage. Jesko, he wrote, had been stupid enough to be drunk as a skunk at Greetsiel harbour late on Tuesday night and run into him.

That's when I saw red and grabbed a rusty cleat that was lying loose on the quay and I pulled it over his head. Once for Gina, once for Talea and then again for all the shit he did to other people.

He had only wanted to beat Jesko up, but not to kill him.

In the end, however, the blows with the cleat were probably stronger than intended.

Well aware that Büttner knew as much about seafaring as he did about manned space travel, Hasenkrug had kindly added the explanation that cleats on ships and in the harbour were used for mooring ropes.

Eiko then dragged the dead Jesko on board the cutter with which he and his crew wanted to set sail the next morning. On the high seas, he had let the body go overboard unnoticed in the dark.

Never in my life would I have expected Jesko's body to get caught in a fishing net, and then in my father's, of all things.

Although he was no longer alive, Jesko had ultimately remained the victor, because he had once again achieved what had always been his purpose in life: to destroy the lives of other people.

Eiko Harms' letter ended with a few parting words to his parents and siblings and, at the very end, with the request: *Don't be angry with me.*

"So he actually threw himself into the North Sea off Helgoland?" inquired Susanne, who was clearing the table after dinner.

"Yes, it looks like it. In the end, he was probably a seaman with body and soul," Büttner remarked. "One of our colleagues told us that Eiko Harms had mentioned time and again recently that only a grave on the high seas would be an option for him when he died. So it was probably only logical that he now chose this path."

"He must have been desperate," Susanne noted.

"He knew that sooner or later we would find out about him. So he chose suicide over prison."

Susanne shook her head. "Terrible story. So many young people who lost their lives. And so many people who are now mourning them."

"Then there are those who have to come to terms with the fact that they will go to prison for manslaughter because Jesko bluntly told them a lie," growled Büttner. "And then there are those young women who could at any time encounter some lecher on the street who got off on their sex with Jesko Mudder, and who might recognise them."

Susanne shuddered. "I don't even like to imagine what something like that would have done to Jette."

At the latest after this remark, Büttner was convinced that the line between being a peace-loving person and being a murderer was often a very thin one. He, too, would by no means put his hand in the fire that he would not do the same out of revenge for his daughter as Eiko Harms had done for his girlfriend and his sister. But of course, as a homicide detective, he could not say that out loud.

"Speaking of Jette," Susanne said after glancing at her watch. "Five minutes until the arranged call. I'll switch on the laptop."

Büttner's mood rose considerably when he saw his daughter in high spirits a little later. She was sitting in light summer clothes on Debbie's little terrace in the shade, and her skin had already turned a little colour.

"I had my first lesson at the language school today," Jette reported. "It's a very small school where Debbie also teaches. I have already met so many great people there who come from all over the world that I am totally flashed. It's all even much, much better than I imagined."

"And have you already found out what else there is to do in Cape Town and the surrounding area?" inquired Susanne.

"Sure. But it's so endless that I can't even list it all." Jette looked up, then lifted her laptop so that her parents could now see not her, but exclusively bright blue sky. "Do you see that?" exclaimed Jette excitedly. She briefly pushed her face, beaming with enthusiasm, in front of the camera, then she was gone again.

"What?" asked Büttner and Susanne at the same time, for nothing showed itself to them except a deep blue.

The picture panned around and Jette's face came back into view. "Paragliding," she said. "There are paragliders up in the sky."

Büttner frowned. "Aren't these the madmen who throw themselves down into the valley from some mountain or other?"

Jette rolled her eyes. "Oh, Pops, the way you say it, it sounds like they're throwing themselves to their deaths on purpose. But yes, they are paragliders."

Susanne made a dismissive gesture with her hand. "You know your father wasn't exactly born an adventurer, Jette. He already calculates the probability of derailing the Borkum small railway when he boards it."

"Anyway," Jette picked up the thread again, "the paragliders come from Signal Hill, fly a curve over the sea and then land right on the promenade."

"And what exactly is so exciting about these paragliders?" Büttner wanted to know, not understanding Jette's enthusiasm.

"Everything," was Jette's reply. "Simply everything, Pops. And from tomorrow I'll be one of them."

"Um… what?" Büttner hoped he had misheard.

"You actually want to try it?" asked Susanne, ignoring her husband.

"Yes," Jette replied, to Büttner's horror. "And if I like it – which I assume I will – I want to learn it myself. After all, I've been here long enough."

"Your father looks a little distressed. Is everything okay?" Debbie waved briefly at the camera, but made no move to join them, disappearing from the picture immediately afterwards.

Yes, he was distressed, and no, nothing was okay. While Susanne and Jette simply dismissed Debbie's question with a smile and a wave of the hand, Büttner wondered if it wouldn't be a good plan to get on the plane to Cape Town to check things out.

Dear reader

I am very pleased that you have chosen "Howling offshore" to read and I hope that I have been able to give you a few pleasant hours with this crime novel. In this case, I would be very pleased to receive a review or feedback by e-mail (mail@elke-bergsma.de).

It is always an honour for me to include real people in my books. This time was no exception. To make this possible, however, I had to send Jette on a journey – and make Büttner suffer a little.

The real person in "Howling offshore" is a woman I have grown very fond of named Debbie, who has accompanied me for two years now, although unfortunately mostly only via Zoom. In the spring of this year, however, I had the fortune to finally meet Debbie in person in her hometown of Cape Town. And that's how the idea for sideshow and side character came about, to which I equally lost my heart in the spring. A thousand thanks, dear Debbie, for agreeing to be part of my story!

And since we're chatting so nicely about Debbie: If you, dear reader, ever feel the need to improve your English or just practise it so it doesn't get rusty: Write to me! I'll be happy to refer you to Debbie, because she's also an English teacher in real life (including mine, hence the Zoom calls ☺), and a wonderful one at that.

Another big thank you goes to my editor Kanut Kirches (www.lektorat-kanut-kirches.de), who stepped in very spontaneously for "Howling offshore" and played a good part in making this crime novel what it is now with valuable comments, objections, suggestions and constructive criticism.

Corinna Rindlisbacher (www.ebokks.de) converted the text file into the correct format. Many thanks for that!

I am very pleased with the successful cover, which was once again designed by Susanne Elsen (www.mohnrot.com). Thank you!

And now guess who did the proofreading for this English version! That's right, it was Debbie. I say a big thank you to her for that too!

Best regards
Elke Bergsma

www.elke-bergsma.de
www.facebook.com/elkebergsmaautorin
www.instagram.com/bergsmaautorin